We're back and more hard-boiled than ever.

Call us self-serving, but this time we'd like to thank some of the critics who've supported Old School Books. In case you missed it, here's what a few of them had to say:

Spin: "Walking the mean streets with hearts set on dreams they know damn well they'll never reach, these authors keep it realer than any rapper knows how. . . . They testify to how much was lost when these novelists couldn't get read as seriously as they should have."

The Source: "They take the brutality and ruin of the urban black landscape and transform them into art."

Playboy: "One of the most exciting literary revival series since the rediscovery of Jim Thompson's novels."

Detour: "The Old School will give the modern reader a wake-up slap, alerting them to a subversive canon too long ignored."

Details: "Down-and-dirty tales about real O.G.'s, stories that drop you in the middle of the crumbling inner cities for a street-level view of the black urban experience. . . . If you like the page-turning pulp of Raymond Chandler, James Ellroy, and Jim Thompson, definitely add the Old School to your hard-boiled syllabus."

Time Out: "Unflinching biographies of the streets. . . . a blood-soaked landmark of crime fiction."

USA Today: "Harder than a set of brass knuckles and pulpier than home-squeezed orange juice. . . . With any luck the legacy of the Old School Books writers will not be lost again."

New York Newsday: "The editors have unearthed a motherload of revelation; a shadow tradition of hot-wired prose playing its own variations on noir with bebop abandon and rhythm-and-blues momentum."

Kind words, and don't think we aren't grateful.

While we've got your attention, we'd like to make this important announcement. OSB will soon unveil its first hardcover reissue:

Chester Himes's lost classic, *Cast the First Stone*. Least that's what the world has called it until now. With a little help from some friends, we've restored one hundred (or so) pages from Himes's original manuscript, "dyed" several of the characters black as they were in Himes's earliest editions, and are publishing it under its original title, *Yesterday Will Make You Cry*. We consider it nothing less than a literary revelation—we hope you will too.

Until then, we hope you enjoy our terrific trio of new titles. And be sure to keep those cards and letters coming.

Daddy Cool

OLD SCHOOL BOOKS

edited by Marc Gerald and Samuel Blumenfeld

Daddy Cool

DONALD GOINES

Old School Books

W · W · Norton & Company
New York · London

The text of this book is composed in Sabon, with the display set in Staccato 555 and Futura.
Composition by Crane Typesetting Service, Inc.
Manufacturing by Courier Companies, Inc.
Book design by Jack Meserole.

Library of Congress Cataloging-in-Publication Data

Goines, Donald, 1937-1974.
    Daddy Cool / Donald Goines.
        p.   cm. — (Old school books)
    ISBN 0-393-31664-5 (pbk.)
    I. Title.   II. Series.
PS3557.03255D33   1997
813'.54—DC21   97—358
                                                                    CIP

W. W. Norton & Company, Inc., 500 Fifth Avenue, New York, NY 10110
www.wwnorton.com

W. W. Norton & Company Ltd., 10 Coptic Street, London WC1A 1PU

3 4 5 6 7 8 9 0

Dedicated to

*my main man and his out-of-sight lady, Rickie,
a tall, fine black sister who steps so fast that
the only thing she has to worry about running
second to is a mean-ass jet plane.
The brother who is just as swift as his woman
is the cool and always mellow Kenny.
Here's wishing you good luck in any endeavor
you and your lady might undertake.
And I'd also like to wish the best of fortune
to Kenny's beautiful sister Shirley,
who also happens to be a
very proud and lovely black lady.*

DONALD GOINES

Donald Goines's life ended abruptly in Detroit in 1974 just miles from his childhood home. He was shot to death while at his typewriter as he was putting the final touches on his seventeenth novel, *Kenyatta's Last Hit*. It was a tragic end, to be sure, but somehow fitting for a writer whose greatest gift was his ability to search his memory and tell the story of how his neighbors lived and died.

Goines was born in 1937 and was primed to take over his family's laundry shop. But while still in his teens, he ditched school, lied about his age, and took up with the Air Force. He returned home from Japan in 1955 a full-time heroin addict.

For the next fifteen years, Goines supported his addiction robbing and pimping, gambling and stealing, and was in and out of jail seven times. During his final stretch at the Jackson Penitentiary, a facility in which fellow Old School scribe Clarence Cooper, Jr., had served a decade earlier, he decided to try his hand at writing Westerns. Without much luck. Introduced to the writings of Robert "Iceberg Slim" Beck, a pimp-novelist who was incredibly popular behind bars, Goines found the perfect model for the kind of black-experience tales he wanted to tell.

Still incarcerated, Goines wrote *Whoreson*, a semiautobiographical account of the son of a prostitute who grows up to become a pimp. He followed it up with *Dopefiend*, a raw, sordid chronicle of two black middle-class girls' descent into the nightmarish world of addiction. There are no heroes to be found here—these are not remakes of *Shaft*. Like all of Goines's best books, each reveals the darker and truer side of reality where the common experience shared by all is pain.

Both works—along with the entire Goines oeuvre—were published by Holloway House, the same Los Angeles company that put out Iceberg Slim. It was a perfect match. Sold in cut-rate paperback editions in mom-and-pop, black America, they found an instant audience.

Released from jail in 1970, Goines had a lot of making up to do, and he spent the rest of his life in a creative, compulsive fever. His schedule was relentless, and methodical as Hemingway's. Writing in the morning, shooting up the rest of the day, he somehow managed to turn out as many as eight books a year. Their number included gritty, graphic accounts of crooked deals, pimps, and gangsters and the more politically charged Kenyatta series, which he published under the name Al C. Clark.

In the years since his death, Goines's novels have gained increasing influence in the hip-hop nation and are said to sell even better today than they did during his short, creative life. Indeed, it was recently reported that his total sales were now approaching 10 million copies. Domestically, however, critical recognition has been minimal, and white readership has been virtually nonexistent. Ironically, perhaps, the French have embraced Goines with the kind of fervor and reverence they bestow only on the greatest American icons. With the translation of *Whoreson* in 1993, Goines was compared to Jean-Jacques Rousseau; with the release of *Dopefiend*, he was heralded as the greatest black American writer since Chester Himes.

Daddy Cool isn't one of Goines's best-known novels, but it is surely one of his best. It reveals a literary breadth and stylistic intensity often overlooked amid all the bodies and bullets. The ultimate Shakespearean revenge fantasy, it is also unbridled ghetto realism at its best.

Daddy Cool

1

LARRY JACKSON, BETTER known as "Daddy Cool," stopped on the litter-filled street in the town of Flint, Michigan. His prey, a slim, brown-complexioned man, walked briskly ahead. He was unaware that he was being followed by one of the deadliest killers the earth had ever spawned.

Taking his time, Daddy Cool removed a cigarette pack and lit up a Pall Mall. He wasn't in a hurry. He knew that the frightened man in front of him was as good as dead. Whenever the man glanced back over his shoulder he saw nothing moving on the dark side of the street.

William Billings let out a sigh of relief. He had gotten away with it. Everybody had talked about how relentless the number barons were that he worked for, but after ten years of employment with the numbers men, he had come to the conclusion that it was just another business. Like the well-talked-about Mafia, the black numbers men he worked for depended on their reputations to carry them along. And many of those frightening stories out of the past became so outrageous that separating reality from unreality often was impossible.

Five years ago William had formulated the idea of how to rip off the people he worked for, but it had taken him another five years to get up the nerve to really put his dream to work. It had been easier than he imagined. The money had just been lying there waiting for him to pick it up. Actually, he was the accountant, so every day he was in contact with at least ten thousand dollars in cash. The problem lay with faking out the two elderly women who worked in the storefront with him. William had to hold back a burst of laughter when he went back over the events and how simple it had been. All those years of waiting, being afraid of what might happen if he walked out with the money, had made him ashamed. He could have ripped off the money five years earlier and been in South America by now, with his dream ranch producing money. But out of fear he had waited. Now that he had done it, he realized that all the waiting had been in vain. It had only been his inborn fear that had kept him from being rich.

A young girl in her early teens walked past, her short skirt revealing large, meaty thighs. William did something he never did. He spoke to the young girl as she went past, her hips swaying enticingly.

The girl ignored the older, balding man, keeping her head turned sideways so that she didn't have to look into his leering eyes.

At any other time the flat rejection would have filled William with a feeling of remorse. But now, because of the briefcase he carried, it didn't faze him at all. He even managed to let out a contemptuous laugh. The silly fool, he coldly reflected. If she had only known that I carried enough money in this briefcase to make every dream she ever had come true, she wouldn't have acted so funky. He laughed again, the sound carrying to the young girl as she hurried on her way home. At the sound of William's laughter, she began to walk faster. His laughter seemed to be sinister in the early evening darkness that was quickly falling. The sudden appearance of another man from around a parked car gave the girl a fright, but after another quick glance, she forgot about him. It was obvious that the man wasn't paying any attention to her. She glanced back once at the tall black man, then hurried on her way.

At the sight of the young girl coming down the street, Daddy Cool pulled his short-brimmed hat farther down over his eyes. He didn't want anyone recognizing him at this particular moment.

At the sound of Billings' voice, Daddy Cool relaxed. If William could find anything to laugh about at this stage of the game, it showed that the man was shaking off the fear that had made him so cautious earlier in the day. Now it was just the matter of the right opportunity presenting itself. Then Daddy Cool would take care of his job and be on his way home in a matter of moments.

At the thought of home, a slight frown crossed Larry's face. His wife would be cuddled up in the bed watching the television at this time of night. Janet might be anywhere. Without him at home she would surely run wild, staying out to daybreak before coming home, because she knew her mother would be sound asleep by the time she came in. And even if she was awake, there was nothing to fear because she wouldn't say anything to her about keeping late hours. All she was interested in was having a cold bottle of beer in her hand and a good television program. That was what made her happy.

Larry frowned in the dark as he wondered about the tricks fate could play on a man. He remembered the first time he had seen his wife. She had been dancing with a group at a nightclub. How he had wished he could make her his woman. Now, twenty years later, after getting the woman he had dreamed about as a young man, he realized just how foolish he had been. Instead of choosing a woman for her brains, he had foolishly chosen one because of the way she was built. The last fifteen years had been lived regretting his ignorance.

Even as he followed this line of thought, he realized that he would have put her out long ago if it hadn't been for his daughter, Janet. Knowing how it was to grow up as a child without any parents, he had sworn to raise any children born to him. Janet had been the only child born out of his marriage. So he had poured out all his love for his only child, giving Janet whatever she thought about having. He had spoiled the girl before she was five years old. Now that she was in her teens, he couldn't remember when either one of them had ever whipped the child. Janet had grown up headstrong and used to having her way. Because of the money Daddy Cool made, it hadn't bothered him. Whatever the child had ever wanted, he had been able to give it to her.

Daddy Cool noticed the man he was following turn the corner and start walking faster. There was no better time than now to make the hit. As long as the man stayed on these back streets it would be perfect. He only had to catch up with the man without arousing his suspicions. Daddy Cool started to lengthen his stride until he was almost running.

William had a definite goal. A longtime friend stayed somewhere in the next block, but over the years he had forgotten just where the house was. In his haste to leave Detroit, he had left his address book on the dining-room table, so it was useless to him now. He slowed down, knowing that he would recognize the house when he saw it. It was on Newal Street, that he was sure of. It shouldn't be too hard to find in the coming darkness.

Like a hunted animal, Billings' nerves were sharpened to a peak. Glancing back over his shoulder, he noticed a tall man coming around the corner. His first reaction was one of alarm. His senses, alert to possible danger, had detected the presence of someone or something in the immediate vicinity. As a shiver of fear ran down his spine, he ridiculed himself for being frightened of his own shadow. There was no need for him to be worried about someone picking up his trail. Not this soon anyway.

Disregarding the warning alarm that went off inside his head, he slowed his pace so that he could see the old shabby houses better. The neighborhood had once been attractive, with the large rambling homes built back in the early twenties. But now, they were crumbling. Most of them needed at least a paint job. Where there had once been rain gutters, there were now only rusted-out pieces of tin, ready to collapse at the first burst of rain.

William cursed under his breath. He wondered if in his early haste he might have made a wrong turn. It was possible. It had been years since he'd been up this way, and it was easy for him to get turned around. He slowed his walk down until he was almost standing still. Idly he listened to the footsteps of the man who had turned down the same street as he did. Unable to control himself, William turned completely around and glanced at the tall, somberly dressed man coming toward him. He let out a sigh as he realized that he had been holding his breath. He noticed that the man coming toward him was middle-aged. Probably some family man, he reasoned, hurrying home from work. He almost laughed out loud as he reflected on what a hired killer would look like. He was sure of one thing, a hit man wouldn't be as old as the man coming toward him. In his mind, William pictured the hit man sent out after him as a wild young man, probably in his early twenties. A man in a hurry to make a name for himself. One who didn't possess too high an intelligence, that being the reason he would have become a professional killer. It didn't take any brains to pull the trigger on a gun, William reasoned. But a smart man would stay away from such an occupation. One mistake and a hit man's life was finished.

Suddenly William decided that he was definitely going the wrong way. He whirled around on his heels swiftly. The tall, light-complexioned man coming near him stopped suddenly. For a brief moment William hesitated, thinking he saw fear on the man's face. The dumb punk-ass bastard, William coldly reflected. If the sorry motherfucker only knew how much cash William had in the briefcase he carried, the poor bastard wouldn't be frightened by William's sudden turn.

"Don't worry, old chap," William said loudly so that the other man wouldn't fear him. "I'm just lost, that's all. These damn streets all look alike at night."

The tall, dark-clothed man had hesitated briefly; now he came forward quickly. He spoke softly. "Yeah, mister, you did give me a fright for just a minute. You know," he continued as he approached, "you can't trust these dark streets at night. Some of these dope fiends will do anything for a ten-dollar bill."

William laughed lightly, then smiled. He watched the tall man reach back behind his collar. Suddenly the smile froze on his face as the evening moonlight sparkled brightly off the keen-edged knife that was twitching in the man's hand.

Without thinking, William held out his hand. "Wait a minute," he cried out in fear. "If it's money you want, I'll give you all mine." Even in his fright, William tried to hold on to the twenty-five thousand dollars he had in his briefcase. He reached for the wallet in his rear pocket. He never reached it.

With a flash, the tall man dressed in black threw his knife. The motion was so smooth and quick that the knife became only a blur. The knife seemed to turn in the air once or twice, then became imbedded in William's slim chest. It happened so suddenly that William never made a sound. The force of the blow staggered him. He remained on his feet for a brief instant while the knife protruded from his body.

With a quiet groan, William Billings began to fall. The pavement struck him in the back. His eyes were open slightly as he felt more than saw the silent man bending down over him. He tried to open his eyes wider as he felt the knife being withdrawn. Why? he wanted to ask, but the question never formed on his lips. The cold steel against his neck was the last thing he felt on this earth. When the tall, light-complexioned man stood up with the briefcase hanging limp from his left hand, William Billings never heard the quiet words the man spoke.

"You should have never tried to take it, friend," Daddy Cool said as he leaned down and wiped the blood off his favorite dagger. He liked to use the knives whenever he could. They were quieter and less trouble. He glanced back over his shoulder to see if anybody had noticed the silent affair. The streets were still deserted as the cool evening breeze began to blow.

Without another glance, Daddy Cool stepped to the curb and quickly crossed the street. His long strides took him away from the murder scene quickly. He walked briskly but not so much in a hurry as to draw attention. When he reached the corner, he took a backward glance and for the first time noticed an old black woman coming down the steps from the shabby house where the body lay.

At the sight of him peering back at her, she hesitated and stood where she was.

"Damn!" The curse exploded from Daddy Cool's lips as his jaw muscles drew tight. The old bitch had probably been watching the whole thing from her darkened windows. But, Daddy Cool reasoned as he continued on his way, it had been too dark for her to see anything. No matter. He began to move swiftly now toward his car, which was parked two blocks away on another side street.

Daddy Cool turned down the next block and silently cut through somebody's yard. He walked quietly, listening for dogs. His luck held as he made it through the yard and didn't run into any dogs until he started to cut through a yard that he was sure would bring him out near his car. Now his mind was busy. He wondered if the old bitch had called the police before coming out and trying to give aid to a dead man. If she had, they would be setting up lookouts for a man on foot. He couldn't take any more chances.

The large, muscular German police dog jumped up on the fence and barked loudly. Daddy Cool took a quick glance at the house and noticed that it was dark. There was the chance that everybody was sound asleep, but he doubted it. They were more than likely watching television. He started to walk down to the next yard but instantly saw that the yard contained two large mongrel dogs. Without hesitating, Daddy Cool retraced his steps.

Again the large German police dog jumped up against the fence, barking loudly. Suddenly his bark stopped and the dog toppled back on the ground with the handle of the long dagger sticking out of his neck. Daddy Cool took the time to retrieve his knife. He couldn't leave it. It was like a calling card. If the police found his knife they would know that a professional had been at work. Over the past years, he had had to leave his knives on three different occasions. His knives were handmade by him in his own basement, so that there was no way of tracing the knives back to any stores. But the police in three different cities had his knives, waiting for a day when they would be able to tie them with the killer who so boldly used them. For the past ten years certain detectives followed up all knife killings such as the one that had been committed tonight. With patience they slowly waited until one day the killer would make a mistake.

Daddy Cool didn't have the slightest intention of making that mistake. The thought of driving all the way back home with the telltale knife in his possession was a grim thought. If the police should stop him and find the knife, he would be busted. As he crossed the yard silently he removed his handkerchief and wiped the knife clean. Then, seeing that the back steps of the porch were open, he leaned down and tossed the knife and hankie under the house as far as he could.

Without seeming to have stopped, he continued on his silent

way, coming out on the sidewalk and quickly walking past two houses to where his black Ford was parked. He tossed the briefcase on the seat beside him and started up the car motor. Glancing up, he saw the headlights of a car turn down the block, and he quickly cut his motor off and stretched out on the car seat. As soon as he heard the car pass, he raised up and watched until the headlights disappeared completely before restarting his own car.

He pulled out onto the deserted street and drove silently toward the main street, which would lead eventually to the highway.

IT TOOK LESS THAN an hour after arriving back in Detroit for Daddy Cool to take care of his business. The first thing he did was to drop off the briefcase with the twenty-five thousand dollars. He received his ten-thousand-dollar payment for the contract, then started for home. It was three o'clock in the morning when he turned off Seven Mile Road and drove slowly down Ripelle Street. The neighborhood was still mixed but was quickly becoming predominantly black. The homes were well taken care of because the blacks in the neighborhood had paid top dollar to purchase the high-priced homes from the fleeing whites. The well-kept lawns gleamed brightly in the moonlight.

Daddy Cool had a feeling of pride as he drove slowly up to his expensive ranch-style home. He had it built from the ground up, after first putting his money into a poolroom so that he could give the appearance of being a smart businessman. He had been around too long to fall into the trap that many of the other money-hungry blacks fell into: buying high-priced homes with no apparent means of support.

The circular driveway was always a source of pride to him, but now, as he pulled into it, his lips tightened into a snarl. The long, powder-blue Cadillac parked in front of the carport brought his anger to the boiling point. He knew at once who the car belonged to. It was one of the young boys in the neighborhood who thought of himself as a pimp. Many times Daddy Cool had sat in his pool-room and listened to this same young man talk about his exploits with the young girls of the neighborhood. Now the young man was spending his time with Janet, Daddy Cool's young daughter. He had warned the girl about the boy, but she hadn't paid any attention to him, thinking he was just being old-fashioned. She loved the attention she received when she and the self-proclaimed pimp rode through the neighborhood with the top down.

Pulling up behind the car, Daddy Cool sat quietly behind the wheel, using the time to gain some control of his temper. He had never let any of his children see him in a rage, and he had no intention of losing it now. He remembered his only close friend, Big Earl, begging him to let him handle the young punk who was so disrespectful. Daddy Cool had laughingly put the massive black man off. Earl was several inches taller than Daddy Cool, who himself stood over six feet. As Daddy Cool thought about his friend's quiet request, he couldn't help picturing the massive black with his over-sized head. Even for his huge body, Earl's head was too large—it was deformed and roughly the girth and shape of a young water-melon. His eyes were bulbous and froglike. A vivid pale scar ran from his forehead to his neck, cutting his face into two unequal halves. Both of his ears had missing lobes, and what remained had healed unevenly.

The man was grotesque, to say the least, and he brought fear to many who saw him for the first time. His only desire was to serve Daddy Cool, who gave him a place to stay behind the poolroom and a job that kept him off the streets. For that his loyalty was complete. He would freely give his life for the tall, light-complexioned man who accepted him so freely without question.

Now the thought of this man's desire to take care of the young pimp named Ronald brought a slight smile to Daddy Cool's face, but he didn't really need Big Earl to do anything for him. He could take care of Ronald himself. If he ever made up his mind to do it.

As he stared ahead at the parked Cadillac, he knew the boy had seen his headlights when he pulled up. But Ronald had made no attempt to pull out of his way. Instead, Ronald had wrapped his arms around Janet and kissed her slowly. Finally, having watched too much, Daddy Cool pressed down on his horn, blowing it loudly as he again fought down his boiling temper. The young pimp was thoroughly unlikable. He seemed to go out of his way to antagonize Daddy Cool.

With slow deliberation, Ronald started the motor of his car as Janet jumped out on the passenger side. She waved and smiled brightly at Ronald, then whirled around on her heels. Her lips came down into a frown and Daddy Cool knew that she was angry. He took a quick glance at his watch and noticed that it was almost three-thirty in the morning. That was one hell of a time for a girl just sixteen to be coming home. Although she was on the verge of turning seventeen, she was still a child to him.

Janet waited with her hands on her hips while her father pulled up and parked under the car shed. Daddy Cool sighed as he got out. His anger was going to be his downfall one day if he didn't learn to control it better. Even as he approached the girl he cautioned himself about his anger. His temper was already almost out of control and he didn't really know how much he could take. From the happenings of the past night's work, he was still keyed up to a high pitch. He tried to slow himself down.

"Well!" Janet snarled like a young jungle cat. Her bright teeth gleamed in the moonlight. She was a bewitching picture standing there with her hands on her hips. Her hair was long and silky, running down to her shoulders like shining black silver. Her face had a golden tone to it, more Mexican than Negro. Her lips were thin, like her father's, and she had the same leaping black eyes, which looked like those of wild hawks with their eyes gleaming under the moonlight.

"You know you didn't have to do that, Daddy," she began. "We knew it was you pulling up behind us. Ronald only wanted to say goodnight to me without pulling away at your sudden appearance as if he was frightened. I mean, he's a man, too, even if he is much younger than you."

It wasn't so much the words she used that hurt him, it was the tone of voice. She spoke to him as if she was scolding a child. Before he knew what he was doing, his hand came up and knocked her to the ground. She stared up at him in surprise. This was the first time he had ever put his hands on her, and she couldn't believe that it had happened. Before she could say anything sassy, he reached down and jerked her to her feet.

"Hear this, little bitch," he growled, and he didn't recognize his own voice. "If you ever try speakin' to me in that tone of voice again, I'll kick your ass so hard you won't be able to sit sideways in that goddamn Caddie, you understand?"

Before she could shake her head one way or the other, his hand moved in a blur. Twice he slapped her viciously across the face. Her scream came out shrilly at first, then louder. He twisted her around and gave her a violent shove toward the front door.

"And another thing, Miss Fine, as long as you live under this goddamn roof, you had better make sure that motherfuckin' door hits you in the crack of your ass before twelve o'clock at night," he stated, then added, "Do I make myself clear?"

Janet could only shake her head. She was too frightened to speak. She had never really seen the man who was walking swiftly behind her. This wasn't the soft old man she could bend around her fingers like putty. No, this was another person, one whom she had never seen before. For the first time in her life she feared the man who had always been dear to her. She trembled as she hurried toward the front door. With shaking hands, she inserted her key and quickly opened the front door.

Tears ran freely from her eyes as she staggered across the threshold. As Daddy Cool entered, the first thing he noticed was his wife, to whose arms Janet had fled.

"Oh, Mother," she cried over and over again.

"Now, now, child," Daddy Cool's wife, Shirley, said. "It's okay, honey. Everything is all right." Her eyes sought out those of her husband. The sounds from in front of their house had awakened her, but she had no knowledge of what had happened to her daughter.

"He struck me," Janet finally managed to say, as large tears ran down both her cheeks. A sob caught in her throat as she remembered the vivid scene that had just transpired.

Shirley was dumbfounded. She didn't have the slightest idea who her daughter was talking about. It never even entered her mind that Daddy Cool was the one she was referring to.

"Larry," Shirley said, addressing her husband sharply, "what is the child talking about?"

"She tryin' to tell you that I slapped her," Larry Jackson stated, as he stared cold-eyed at his wife.

"What!" Shirley exclaimed loudly, unable to catch up with the conversation. She couldn't believe what she had heard.

"I said she is tryin' to pull your coat that I slapped the shit out of her," Daddy Cool stated harshly.

"You slapped her?" Shirley murmured over and over again. Even now that the words were out, Shirley still couldn't believe what she had heard.

"That's right," he stated again. "If you had taken care of your responsibilities like you should have, this wouldn't have been necessary. I told you before I left to stay on this kid's ass and make her come home early!"

"Shit!" The word came out louder than she had intended. Shirley dropped her eyes. She didn't like the cold gleam that came into her man's jet black eyes. "I mean, Larry, you know she won't mind me. Hell, if she won't mind you, how the hell do you expect me to make her mind me?"

With firm hands Shirley slowly disengaged herself from her daughter.

"Okay now, Janet, it's all right. It won't kill you. Maybe it might slow you down some, though." She gently pushed her daughter away.

Finally Janet stopped crying. The tears stopped flowing and anger began to overwhelm her. For the first time in her young life she was speechless. She had been slapped, and to her that was something unheard of. As the thought of what had happened dawned on her, her cheeks became red with a futile anger.

"Mother," she began, then didn't really know what she wanted to say.

"Larry," Shirley said, "don't you think it's a late date to start using a strong hand on her?"

"Not as long as she keeps her young ass in my house," Daddy Cool stated harshly, his anger still not completely under control.

"Well, that's not so difficult to handle," Janet replied, sparks of fire leaping in her cold black eyes.

"What do you mean by that?" he asked softly. The gentleness of his voice hadn't fooled Shirley. She had lived with the man too long. She knew his moods almost as well as he did. She tried to catch her daughter's eye so that she could warn Janet, but the young girl was now in open rebellion. With her mother near, she believed she didn't have any reason to fear her father. What had happened outside would never occur in front of Shirley.

"What I mean," Janet said contemptuously, "is that I don't just have to live here. I can easily find me a small apartment somewhere." She shook her head quickly, tossing the hair back out of her face.

"And just how the hell do you expect to pay the rent, may I ask?" Daddy Cool asked quietly, watching his daughter closely. Each word she said seemed to burn inside his head.

"That shouldn't be too hard either," Janet stated coldly, her face flushed with anger.

"I suppose you think that punk Ronald is going to pay your rent for you, huh?" Daddy Cool inquired.

"He just might at that," she said in a sassy manner, while her mother let out a gasp.

"Larry," Shirley interrupted, "let's let this thing ride until morning. Maybe after we sleep on it we can talk about it with less heat, okay?" She stared from one face to the other. They were so much alike, she reflected. Each one was strong-willed and neither one would willingly give in. If only she could think of some way to get them away from the conversation. Shirley saw the danger that loomed ahead, while her husband was too angry to realize that he was driving his daughter up a one-way street with no way of getting back.

Daddy Cool let out a sharp laugh. "Yeah, I'll just bet he'll pay out cash money for a place for you. By the time you finished selling ass each and every night, you'd have made enough money to pay the rent of a penthouse!"

Janet let out a gasp. "Is that what you think?" She stared at her father with hatred. "You don't think no better of me than that," she stated again, not really believing the words she heard.

"It's not you I believe in. It's that funky nigger you think you're playin' around with. He ain't nothing but a petty-ass pimp, so what makes you think you'll be treated any better than the rest of his girls?" Daddy Cool asked coldly, his jet black eyes flashing their anger.

Janet whirled around on her heels and stalked off toward her bedroom. Her stepbrother Jimmy stood in her path. There was a smile on his lips, revealing that he had overheard most of the conversation.

"Would you mind getting out of my way?" she scowled in a scorching voice as she stared coldly at the tall, well-built boy.

"Yes, ma'am," Jimmy said as he bowed from the waist, grinning. "Anything your highness might want. I'se the black boy to do it." He used a southern dialect that he knew would irritate his half sister.

"Get out of her way, Jimmy," Daddy Cool ordered, as he watched the exchange between the teenagers.

"Yes sirreee," Jimmy replied, jumping back quickly.

Shirley let out a sigh as she watched her daughter stalk off. This morning's work wouldn't be soon forgotten, she reflected as she watched Janet's proud back.

Shirley turned to her husband. "Well, Larry, I think you overplayed your hand that time, honey."

Daddy Cool didn't bother to answer. He waited until the girl disappeared, then he hurried to his bedroom.

3

*T*HE SUNLIGHT BEAMING through the framed bedroom window cast rays of gold on the bedspread. Normally, Daddy Cool would have been up by now. One quick look at his diamond-studded watch assured him of the time—it was a little past high noon. For him, it was rare indeed to stay in bed that long. The sunlight generally awakened him early in the morning. Then he would get up and take his morning shower. But today was different. His glance lingered on the ten thousand dollars lying on the dresser top. Most of the time this sight would lift his spirits. But today he couldn't pull his feelings together. Seldom did he allow himself to be down and blue, nor did he like to have anybody around him who was in such a mood. So Daddy Cool remained lying in bed, smoking cigarette after cigarette.

There was a soft knock on the door. "Who is it?" Daddy Cool inquired sharply, more so than he had actually intended.

Shirley hesitated, then spoke up.

"It's me, Larry," she said, then added, "I was wondering if you might like me to fix you something. I could make you a ham sandwich right quick." Her voice was shaking slightly.

Without even thinking about it, he almost dismissed her. Then Daddy Cool remonstrated himself for being so damn evil and changed his mind.

"Okay, Shirley," he replied, trying to make the tone of his voice casual. "I'm gettin' up now, so by the time I take a fast shower, you can lay something out for me. Oh, by the way, honey, if we don't have any, send one of the boys down to the store and pick up some cans of iced tea, okay?"

He didn't wait to hear her reply. Slipping off the bed, he took off his silk shorts and walked naked into the shower. After taking a cold shower he felt a little better. He wondered idly if he was ducking his daughter. He remembered too vividly the events of the early morning. Regret was written across his face as he stared into the mirror. The last thing he should have done, he scolded himself, was to allow his anger to get away from him. Putting his hands on her was the most foolish thing he'd done in years, he thought.

Taking his time, Daddy Cool selected the clothes he would wear for the day. He was an excellent dresser for a man his age. Keeping up with the latest in men's styles, he was always neat. Today he selected a short, light-brown silk shirt, then matched it with a pair of brown pants with large cuffs. Next, he opened the closet where he kept over twenty pairs of shoes.

The latest were those with large heels and he removed a pair that he had only worn once before. The shoes were brown and white, with a four-inch heel. He sprinkled powder inside the shoes before slipping his feet into them. Then he stood up and examined himself in the large bedroom mirror. He could find nothing wrong with his appearance.

He started for the door, then stopped and came back. Picking the stacks of money up from the top of the dresser, he opened his bottom drawer and casually dropped the money into it. After firmly closing it, he departed from the bedroom.

Shirley glanced up, smiling, when he entered the kitchen. The food was already on the table.

"I didn't know if you wanted to eat in here or in the dining room," she stated, as she wondered what kind of mood her man was in this morning.

"It don't make any difference," Larry stated as he pulled out a chair and sat down. He began to eat the ham sandwich, and once he'd done so he realized he was hungry. She watched him eating, then hurried and prepared him another one before he finished with the first. The cold tea had already been poured out of the can and was now in a glass with ice cubes. He drank the tea slowly, enjoying the light meal.

When Shirley bent down and set the food in front of him, Daddy Cool stared down at the well-developed tits that pushed her blouse out so far in the front. He let out a sigh. His woman was still as attractive as ever. She had gained weight, but it looked good on her because it was all in the right places.

Shirley had the same golden brown complexion that their daughter had, and also the beautiful and evenly spaced white teeth—something Daddy Cool knew he lacked. His teeth were disfigured and gaps could be seen whenever he opened his mouth.

"I'm glad to see you're in a better mood than you were this morning," Shirley began, slowly feeling her way. She knew that she had something to tell him, and she realized that once she told him, his anger would shoot up to the boiling point.

"Well, let's just say that's left to be seen," he answered slowly, eyeing his wife closely for the first time that day. Something was on the woman's mind. He believed that he could read her like a book.

Before she could begin, he beat her to the point. "Ain't no sense bullshittin', Shirley. Whatever you got to say, spit it out." He stared at her coldly, knowing that whenever he looked at her in this fashion it upset her. Nevertheless, he didn't make it any easier for her.

Shirley rolled her tongue out and wet her lips, wildly trying to figure out which would be the best way to give her husband the news. Under his sharp stare she became confused and just blurted it out. "Your daughter had a cab pick her up this morning!"

Daddy Cool took a sip from his drink before replying. "So what? It ain't no big thing for her to catch a cab, is it?"

"No, no, not at all," Shirley began, still afraid to add the final words. But then it all came out in a rush. "But this is the first time she took all her clothes with her."

For a minute there was a deadly silence in the kitchen. Shirley could feel herself backing away from the table. The expressions that flashed across her quiet husband's face frightened her. It was rare indeed when she saw him like this.

Once many years ago, when they had first gotten married, a man had accosted them in a bar and ignored Daddy Cool while trying to hold a conversation with her. She had seen that look then, before her husband had cut the man with his straight razor.

Daddy Cool had to repeat himself twice before his wife could understand what he was saying. She was so frightened that it was almost impossible to reach her.

"I said, bitch," he growled, "why the fuck didn't you wake me up and tell me what she was trying to pull off?"

Shirley shook her head in fear. "I didn't know myself, Larry. Jimmy told me about it when I got up. He said she left with three suitcases."

"Jimmy, huh!" Daddy Cool said the name with emphasis. "Just where the hell is Jimmy at now?"

"He went to basketball practice with his brother," she managed to reply.

There was a coldness in the room now and Shirley knew that she didn't have any influence on what her angry husband might do. No matter what she thought, he wouldn't pay the slightest heed to her demands.

Daddy Cool stared coldly at his wife. "I guess you don't really care one way or the other about this shit, do you, Shirley?"

"Of course I care," she answered quickly, "but there's not too much we can do. She'll be seventeen in another month, so we really don't have much control over her movements now. It's just too late, Larry. We should have taken this interest in her activities way before now."

For a brief second Larry felt like slapping his wife's face but realized that it wasn't completely her fault. It was their joint mismanagement of the young girl's affairs that had led to this. Neither one had been firm enough, and now it was damn near too late. But Daddy Cool wouldn't allow himself to even think that it was actually too late.

He believed he could still do something to straighten the matter out. If he could only find her and sit down and have a good talk with her, then she would understand that everything he was doing was for her own good.

With his brain whirling beneath the stunning revelation, Daddy Cool sat rigid, unable to think properly. He couldn't bring his thoughts together; he couldn't make the proper moves.

"It's not just Jimmy's fault," Shirley stated, then added, "Buddy was up and he saw her packing her stuff so he could have awakened you as well as Jimmy."

Without really realizing what he was saying, Daddy Cool replied, "Since Buddy and Jimmy ain't nothing but her half brothers, they both were more than likely glad to see her go. That way," he continued, "they probably hope that they'll be able to get more spending money from me."

Shirley caught her breath. She had known for years that her husband only tolerated her two boys from another man, but this was the first time he had ever said something openly about it. It wasn't what he said, but the way that he said it.

"I guess, then," Shirley began, "it wouldn't make any damn difference to you if Buddy or Jimmy were leaving."

Daddy Cool laughed harshly. "I should say not. Why in the fuck should I be concerned? I've raised them and given them any goddamn thing they ever wanted, so now that both of them are grown, do you think I'd shed tears if they decided to leave?"

He gazed up at her with wide, unseeing eyes. He could only see his young daughter in his mind.

Gradually Shirley fought back the tears that were slowly building. "I don't know why you want to say they're grown. Jimmy is only eighteen, while Buddy is just a year older than that."

The thought raced through Daddy Cool's mind. He pushed his chair back from the table. "If you want to baby them boys, that's up to you. But don't think for a goddamn minute I'm going to baby them also. When I was sixteen I was out on my own, and I think it made a better man out of me for it. Your boys are both spoiled little bastards who are used to havin' their own fuckin' way because I made it easy for them!"

Before she could interrupt, he waved her silent. "Now that my daughter has decided to leave home, there are sure going to be some changes made in this household, you can bet on it."

He stared coldly at his wife, then added, "Before it's over, them two niggers are going to wish like hell they had awakened me this morning. I don't give a fuck what you say, Shirley, I know where I'm coming from. They knew what they were doing when they

31

watched her load her bags into that cab, and you can bet on it. Both of them knew damn well I wouldn't have allowed it, and if they were any kind of brothers they wouldn't have allowed it either!"

When he finished with his outburst, Shirley could only gaze at him, dumbfounded. She knew he was in one of his rare moods and prayed silently that it would pass. Daddy Cool was such a strange man that it was hard to tell what he might do next. If he felt like it, he would put both of his stepchildren out and turn his back on them completely.

As she watched his departing back, she wondered why her two sons had done what they had done. They both knew that their stepfather would be angry over Janet's departure, and that was the main reason they fled from the house. They didn't want to hear his angry voice when he found out. She remembered how Jimmy had laughed while telling her about Janet's leaving. It had been a joke to him, but now it looked as if the joke might turn bitter.

She didn't believe her boys could make it without her or her husband's help. Neither boy had ever held any kind of job, nor had really taken up anything in school that would help them out. Daddy Cool had bought a car for Buddy on his eighteenth birthday and promised one to Jimmy whenever he graduated from school. But Jimmy had quit in his last year so that he could run the streets with his brother.

After leaving the house, Daddy Cool walked to his car and opened the door. He sat behind the steering wheel for a minute before starting up the motor. He didn't want to go to his poolroom but decided that would be the best place to get a line on where his daughter had gone.

If only he could catch up with either one of his stepsons, he was sure they would know where she was.

Daddy Cool backed the car out of the driveway. His mind was so occupied with his thoughts that he almost backed into an oncoming car. The sound of the driver's horn warned him just in time.

It took only five minutes before he was pulling into the rear parking lot of his poolroom. The front of the building advertised the place as "the billiard hall for men and women." A place of leisure. It was not only a poolroom, but catered to other tastes as well. As he let himself in the back door, which was always kept locked, the first thing Daddy Cool did was glance over toward the restaurant section of the hall.

The long counter was empty except for two young girls who were sipping on Cokes as they watched the men in the rear of the place play pool. The restaurant had a long counter plus four heavily padded red booths for people who wanted to eat their food in semi-privacy. The two girls who worked the day shift watched him as he entered. Each one smiled brightly in his direction.

Daddy Cool ignored the waitresses, while his eyes sought out every spot in the place for Janet. The front table that was reserved just for women was empty. Sometimes Janet would spend half a day shooting pool on the women's table.

There were eight tables in the poolroom, but only three of them were in use now. From a high chair that resembled the ones life-guards used out at the public beaches, the massive Earl sat overlooking his domain. He ran the poolroom the way a captain ran a ship. He didn't allow any foul language on the premises, nor drinking.

Many of the neighborhood wineheads had tried slipping wine bottles inside the place, but after the first time they were caught, they never attempted it again. Earl would not accept any apology when he caught people breaking the rules inside the poolroom. One warning was all they got. The next time there was no telling what might happen.

Since Daddy Cool didn't oppose anything Earl did, Earl looked on the poolroom as if it was his own. He was the one who cleaned it out at night after the front doors were closed, going behind the kitchen help and checking on how clean the kitchen was left. Again, he only warned the women who worked once. If they repeated an offense, they had to find another job.

Now, at the sight of his boss's face, Earl knew at once that something was worrying the man. Earl began to frown. His massive watermelon head hung down like a hound dog's. Knowing his boss so well, Earl didn't disturb him with endless questions. He had known that Daddy Cool had left to take care of a contract and wondered if something had gone wrong with the hit. Too much abstract thinking gave him a headache, so he tried to put the worry out of his mind.

If Larry wanted him to know, he would be told in good time. As he raised his huge head and saw Daddy Cool coming toward him, he began to break out into a big smile. He looked like a huge mutt wagging his tail because his master had decided to pat him on the head.

Earl couldn't help himself. He was not a quick-thinking man, and deep inside he was very shy. He knew that many people looked at him as if he was a freak. But ever since Daddy Cool had taken him under his wing and given him a place to stay and work, Earl's world had changed. He didn't have to leave the building for anything. The food his huge body required was right at his fingertips, so he seldom ventured outside to be stared at by the passing people.

Daddy Cool stopped beside the huge man's chair. He rested his arm on his friend's leg, staying in that position for several minutes without speaking. Then Larry raised his eyes and Earl recoiled from all the hurt he saw inside of them. No man should feel like that, Earl reflected, and especially not his only friend. He still remained silent, waiting for Daddy Cool to break the silence.

"She's gone, Earl. Janet done packed her bags and left home," Daddy Cool stated, his voice shaking.

Earl began to fidget. Then, as comprehension dawned on him, his heavily corded neck muscles bulged while he tried to find the proper reply. Before he could say anything, Daddy Cool continued. "Have you heard anything about her whereabouts from any of the boys who come in here?"

Earl shook his head. "Not yet, Larry. But I'm goin' make it a point to find out. When I do, you want me to go on over and collect her up and bring her back home?"

For the first time since getting out of the kitchen, Larry felt relief. With Earl working with him, it wouldn't take them long to run her down. He couldn't understand why he had been so mixed up at first. It was just a matter of waiting for the news to break. As soon as it hit the corner, somebody would come running with it.

"Naw, Earl, that won't be necessary. All you need to do is get in touch with me. After that, I might take you with me, but I don't want you going without me," Daddy Cool stated.

Earl nodded his head in agreement, then got down from his high perch.

"You want to go back to the office and get a hooker?" he inquired, referring to the rear office that he also used as his bedroom.

For a brief second, Daddy Cool hesitated, then agreed. Maybe a strong drink would help settle his nerves while he waited.

JANET LET OUT A SIGH of relief when the cab pulled away from her home. She had been frightened for one of the few times in her life. Upon leaving, she had feared that someone would awaken her father. Jimmy had threatened to do just that if she didn't make it worth his while. So she had dug down into her tiny savings and given him ten dollars. For him to be her half brother was more like a curse.

Over the years she had come to realize that she hated the overbearing brown-skinned boy who was by chance her half brother. Buddy was different. At times she could get along with him, but with Jimmy it was impossible.

She settled back in the cab and gave the driver her destination. At the last minute, she had decided to go and check into a motel until she could reach Ronald. After having tried four different numbers most of the night, she still hadn't been able to reach him.

As the fleeting thought flashed through her mind that he was probably laying up with one of the various whores he bragged about having, she gritted her teeth. Well, in time, she reasoned, she'd see to it that he didn't have any of those kind of women. Her father's remark about Ronald one day having her out on the corner made her blush. For her daddy to even imagine such a thing about her was shocking. She had known that her father had no lost love for Ronald, but she had never believed his dislike was as strong as it was. She was shocked by what had happened in the early morning hours.

To take her mind off the subject, she removed the small wad of bills she had saved in her piggy bank. Slowly Janet counted the money over and over again. She had all of eighty dollars left so, the way she figured it, that should hold her for a few weeks if Ronald didn't do the right thing about her.

But as she thought about it, her doubts left. Ronald loved her, so it shouldn't be such a hard job of convincing him to marry her. Once they got married, all she would have to do would be to lead him down the right road and make him get one of the good jobs in a factory. She sat back and smiled as she pictured herself taking care of their house while Ronald was away working.

How she would surprise him when he came home, having spent most of the day preparing the kind of meal that she knew he would love. Maybe one day, she dreamed as she blushed, they would have a small baby. Then her daddy would forgive her and everything would be all right.

If only her father and Ronald didn't dislike each other so much. She was aware that she was only one of the few people who knew that Ronald really disliked her father. She had never been able to find out just why, but he had a burning dislike for the man everybody called "Daddy Cool."

Ronald laughed whenever he heard this nickname and called her father "Daddy Fool." But in time, she reflected, she might even be able to bring them closer together. Once Ronald really met her father and saw the kindness underneath the cold front that he put out to strangers, they couldn't help but to like each other.

"Well, miss," the driver said, driving into the driveway of the motel she had asked to be taken to, "here you are."

For the first time since her adventure began, Janet hesitated. She had never been inside a motel before in her life. She only knew about this one on Woodward because she passed it every day when she went to school. She was supposed to have gone to school this morning, but that was a problem she would resolve later. She had brought all of her school books along, so it shouldn't be too much of a problem going back once she got this mess straightened out. She thought about her girlfriends and how envious they would be once they learned that she was living on her own.

"Miss?" the driver called.

Again she hesitated. She really didn't know what to do. "Driver," she began, "could I give you the money and pay you to go in and check me into a room. I'll gladly pay you something for your trouble."

The middle-aged black driver glanced back at the young girl. He knew she was young and, from the bags she had, he believed she was leaving home for the first time. He wondered what kind of chance he would have of coming back later on, after he was finished work, and spending a little time with her. She was damn sure pretty.

It had been years since he'd had the chance to fuck a young girl, and one this pretty. He seriously doubted if he had ever had one in his life who looked half as good as she did. He licked his lips, lust flaming in his eyes.

"Well now," he began, "I just might do that for you, if you wouldn't mind my coming back later on and checkin' on you. You know," he added, as he saw anger jump into her eyes, "just to see if you're gettin' along all right."

Janet knew just what the old man had on his mind. She was young but she was far from being a fool. Ever since she was ten she had seen the look in men's eyes whenever they saw her. Now that she was getting older, she saw it more often. And besides, she had heard her brothers talking about it. At times, Ronald had tried putting his hand under her miniskirt, but she had always stopped him, telling him that she wouldn't do anything until after she was married. Ronald only laughed, but the hot flow of desire was in his eyes and hands. When he kissed her, he could hardly control himself. His hands went everywhere.

Suddenly she decided to use the man's lust to her advantage. After all, she reasoned, she didn't have to open the door when he came back.

"That might be all right," she said softly, then added, "How much does one of these rooms cost for the day? Until tomorrow at least?"

The driver rubbed his chin. "I don't know, miss. This early in the morning it's hard to tell. I better go in and find out for you."

He pulled the cab out of the entrance and climbed out. She watched him walk away, a strong distaste filling her mouth. Men were beasts, she reflected, as she stared after him. He was old enough to be her father, yet here he was trying to hit on her.

In a matter of minutes the cab driver was back. He opened the rear door so that he could get a better look at her legs. From the miniskirt she wore, she revealed long, lovely thighs, which filled his mind with lust.

"It's going to cost sixteen dollars, girl," he said, not bothering to take his eyes off her pretty legs. "If you should happen to be short of cash," he managed to say, "I wouldn't mind loaning you what you need."

Again he wet his lips as he imagined laying his gray head down between her soft thighs. He could feel his penis getting hard and, without really realizing it, he dropped his hand down on it.

Janet turned her head away as she fumbled in her purse. "No, that's not necessary. I have enough money to last me," she said and held out a twenty-dollar bill. "I believe that's enough for the room and for your fare. Whatever else is left, you can have it for the trouble you're going through."

He took the money out of her hand, letting his fingers grip her wrist until she almost snatched it out of his grasp. As the man walked away, she could feel herself fighting down the urge to vomit.

Please, Ronald, please, she begged quietly, be home this time when I call.

While waiting for the driver to come back with her key, Janet climbed out of the cab and began to remove her suitcases. She wished she knew which room he was getting for her so that she could start carrying them to it.

The driver returned, swinging a key from his hand. Instead of handing it to her, he picked up two of her bags and walked off, searching for the number. Silently she lifted the remaining bag and followed him. She decided at once that she wouldn't enter the room until he was out of her sight. The room was upstairs on the second landing.

Janet climbed the steps quickly, but first she had to stop and make him go ahead of her. He had wanted to come up behind her, but she was having none of that. She wished now that she had brought the hunting knife her father had given her. In her anger, she had tossed most of the things that weren't necessary on the bed and left them. Most of the articles her father had given her were left at home.

As she followed the man, she remembered the long hours when she was younger that her father had spent with her, teaching her how to throw a knife so that it stuck in the middle of the target. She had become good but had never come close to acquiring the skill her father had. He was uncanny; his ability was incredible. She remembered seeing him hit the bull's-eye ninety-nine times out of a hundred, never being more than an inch off from the main spot.

The cab driver stopped at a room that had "204" on the door. He set the baggage down and opened it. Stepping back, he nodded for her to go in front of him. She stopped and shook her head.

"Could I have my key now?" she inquired in a shaking voice.

She hated the little girl sound she imagined her voice betrayed. Janet held out her hand. They stood that way for a minute or two until the driver shifted his feet, not knowing which way to tackle his problem. He had believed that once he got inside the room with her he might be able to talk her into a little lovemaking.

"Say, honey, suppose I run across the street to the whiskey store and get us a pint, huh?" he asked, coming up with the only way he knew to approach a woman.

"No, thank you," Janet said coldly, still holding out her hand. "I would like very much to get my key from you. I've had a very trying time and now I only want to rest."

"Well, now," he began, "I was thinkin' on them very same lines. I been driving all morning and it would be nice if I stretched out my legs for a while, too."

Finally it dawned on her that being evasive wouldn't do any good. Her cold black eyes became mirrors of black ivory revealing a resemblance to her father. "Mister, I'm tryin' to be nice about it," she said, as she stared into his reddish, weak eyes.

He attempted to grin at her, showing broken and yellowish teeth. "That's what I'm hopin' for, honey, that you'll be nice to an old man," he whined.

Contempt appeared in her eyes as her temper blew. "Listen, you silly old bastard, I'm tryin' to pull your coat nicely, but if that won't do any good, I took your cab number down and if you keep fuckin' with me I'm going to spend a dime and call the police and tell them one of the best lies you ever heard! Now, they might not believe me, but by the time you get through explaining it to them, the cab company you drive for ain't goin' want to hear 'bout nothing you got to say, 'cause I'm under age and you ain't had no reason to come to the motel with me!"

She saw the fear leap into his eyes and continued. "Now, I ain't goin' ask you but one more time to give me my key. I paid for it and I want it without no bullshit!"

The man began to struggle with his anger and fear. Her words had shaken him to his very being. It was easy as hell for her to cause him trouble, he realized at once, and at his age, if he lost this job his ass would be up shit's creek.

"Now, now, young lady, it ain't no reason for you to carry on like that. I didn't mean no harm, none at all," he whined, as he fumbled with the key. He stuck it into her outstretched hand.

40

"That's one hell of a way for you to carry on, girl, after the
I went through for you."

"You got paid for it, didn't you?" she said, still not stepping
into the room.

She stood with her hands on her hips until she saw him go down
the stairway. Then she waited, standing at the rail, until he got in
his cab and started it up. A great feeling of relief overcame her as
she stumbled into the room and slammed the door behind her. She
made sure the lock was on, then fell out across the bed and began
to weep.

Deep sobs escaped from her. Her back rose and fell with the
passion of her tears. Desperately she buried her face in the pillow
and repeated Ronald's name over and over again. It seemed as if
the tears and the repetition of her boyfriend's name gave her some
kind of relief. Eventually she stopped crying and the sweet balm of
sleep overcame her; she drifted off with her tear-streaked cheeks
buried into the soft pillow.

*D*ADDY COOL LISTENED to his wife clearing the breakfast dishes
away from the large dining-room table. Her two sons still sat at
the table, their heads down as they stared silently at the floor.

Pacing back and forth in the living room, Larry stopped and
glared back at the two boys in the dining room. His eyes were bleak
as he took in their crestfallen appearance. For the past half hour
he had been giving both the boys tongue-lashings for their stupidity
in allowing their sister to run away from home.

It had been over a week now since Janet had left, and since

then, Daddy Cool had done something he had never imagined himself doing: he had reported her runaway to the police.

"Now, I'm tellin' you two worthless bastards," Daddy Cool began again, "I want ya out in the streets findin' out where that punk-ass would-be pimp has your sister hid! If you can't find out where she is, find out where he is. If I can find his ass, I'll find out where Janet is stayin', you can bet on that!" Daddy Cool resumed his pacing up and down the long, well-furnished living room.

Buddy, a slim brown-skinned boy with the beginnings of a sandy-colored beard, tried to reason with his stepfather. "Dad, take it easy, man. Don't you know you'll be the first person we'd tell. I mean," he added as he saw his stepfather stop pacing and listen to his words, "it's like this, man. Everybody who knows what's happenin' is keepin' the news from us, 'cause it's common knowledge you're real upset over this shit."

"Upset ain't the word," Jimmy cracked, then regretted his quick retort.

"You better damn well believe upset ain't the word," Daddy Cool stated, glaring angrily at the young boy. "You give me the impression that this is all a big fuckin' joke to you, Jimmy."

Jimmy quickly shook his head, denying what was really the truth. This was the first time in his life he had ever seen anything upset his stepfather, and he enjoyed the older man's discomfort. But common sense told him he had better conceal his enjoyment if he wanted to live at Daddy Cool's house. His mother had already told him that they were walking on dangerous ground, and it wasn't beyond their stepfather's imagination to kick both of them out into the streets.

There was nothing their mother could do about it either, because she had been informed that she could follow them if she felt so inclined. The very thought of the bastard telling his mother some shit like that filled Jimmy with a silent rage that he anxiously concealed.

"Naw," Jimmy answered slowly, "I don't see nothin' funny 'bout none of this. I'm just as worried over Janet's whereabouts as the rest of you."

Daddy Cool stared coldly at the young boy. He couldn't be sure of his suspicions, but if he ever found out that Jimmy actually helped her to get away, there would be hell to pay. The ring of his private telephone came to his ear.

There were two telephones in the house—one everybody could use, and the red one, which stayed in Daddy Cool's bedroom with a lock on it. He never used it to make outside calls. It was there for one reason, so that his private clients could reach him without any delay. Angrily, he stalked off toward his bedroom to answer the telephone.

Buddy glanced over at his younger brother. "You better play it cool, Jimmy, and try to keep that sneer off your face. Daddy Cool ain't playin', man. He's really upset over this shit."

Jimmy glared at his older brother. "Man," he drawled, "fuck Daddy Cool!" The words were low enough so that no one except his brother could overhear them.

Buddy shrugged his wide shoulders. "Okay, smart ass, you make your own bed, so you'll be the one to end up layin' in it," Buddy stated, then added, "As far as I'm concerned, I like livin' here where I'm not bothered about paying rent and buying food. So I'm going to do everything I can to help find Janet. Whatever you do, please keep it to yourself, 'cause I know you ain't got enough sense to get on the winning side."

"What you mean by that?" Jimmy asked sharply.

"You know what I mean," Buddy replied. "Ain't nobody no fool, unless it's you. I got the wire about you ridin' around with Ronald yesterday, man, so don't play games with me. If you've been around Ronald, you know where he's keepin' Janet. In fact, you more than likely have seen her."

Jimmy grinned crookedly. "Aw, man, where you keep gettin' bullshit wires like that, huh?" But it was a fact that he had ridden with Ronald for a little while. The man had wanted to know what Daddy Cool was doing and had paid Jimmy fifty dollars for telling him that Daddy Cool had turned in a missing person's report to the police.

Ronald had cussed and called Daddy Cool all kinds of names, but nevertheless, he had taken precautions after that and made sure that Janet stayed inside. The last thing he wanted was to be busted for having a minor in his company.

Buddy watched his brother's lips pull down into a sneer. "Man," he said sharply, "you think you're doing something slick, Jimmy, but you ain't doing nothing but gettin' ready to fuck yourself up."

Jimmy waved his brother silent. "Dig, Buddy, I know what I'm doing, man. All this shit about Daddy Cool this and Daddy Cool that, it don't mean shit! Maybe ten or fifteen years ago Daddy Cool was somebody, but now he ain't nobody but an old nigger who runs a poolroom."

"You know what, Jimmy?" Buddy stated quietly. "I see now what your problem is. You're just a goddamn fool, that's all. Ain't no way anybody with common sense would make the mistake you're makin' about Daddy Cool."

Jimmy sneered. "Man, fuck that shit! I don't even care to hear about it no more, you dig?"

Buddy just shrugged his shoulders as he stared at his younger brother. He realized there was nothing he could do. Jimmy would just have to learn the hard way. That was the only way he'd get the message.

After leaving the front room, Daddy Cool hurried into his bedroom. Before picking up the telephone he thought about who it might be and knew at once who it was. The same person had called him last night, and he'd turned the job down.

Now, before even picking up the receiver, he was sure it would be Al on the line again. He just didn't want to take no for an answer. If it wasn't for the difficulties he was having at home with his daughter, he would have taken the job, but the way things were now, he knew that his mind wouldn't be completely on his work.

"Hello," he said, cradling the receiver in his neck as he reached in his pocket and got out his smokes. "Yeah, this is me. What's happenin', Al?"

Daddy Cool listened for a second, then stated, "Al, we went through all this shit last night on the phone. If I could have seen my way clear, I would have taken the job then. No, man, it ain't the money. I'm not trying to make you go higher."

After listening for a few minutes, Daddy Cool let out a low whistle.

"Oh boy, you're really tryin' to make it hard for me to get out of this one, ain't you? Goddamn, Al, twenty-five grand is a hell of a lot of money for a job, and I appreciate you offerin' it to me. I tell you what, Al, give me a few hours to think on it. I've got problems at home right now; that's why I don't want to leave town right this minute. But for twenty-five grand, I might have to change my plans."

Daddy Cool hesitated, then continued. "Call me back at four-thirty. By then I'll be able to let you know one way or the other just what I'll do, okay?"

He listened to the man's voice on the other end of the line, then hung up. He smoked his cigarette slowly, thinking about the money he had been offered. It wasn't that he really needed the money, but the idea of passing up such a sweet thing bothered him. Twenty-five grand for a hit was top dollar.

"Goddamn this girl," he cursed out loud. Then, seething with frustration, he ground his cigarette out in the ashtray beside his bed.

For the next hour Daddy Cool argued back and forth with himself, always keeping in mind the amount of money he would lose if he did what his heart wanted him to do: stay at home and find his wayward daughter. Nuts to that shit, he cursed. I'm not about to let any damn girl or woman knock me out of that kind of money.

Determined now to take the job, Daddy Cool picked up the private telephone in his room, only to slam it back down. He stalked out of the bedroom and went into the front room. There he picked up the receiver and dialed the number to his poolroom.

"Hello, Earl," he snapped.

"Yeah, this is Earl," came the reply. For a second, Earl couldn't catch the voice on the other end, but as Daddy Cool began to speak, Earl finally understood.

"Listen, Earl, I'm thinkin' 'bout taking a trip. I got a job I got to handle," Larry stated.

"You want I should go along with you?" Earl asked, his voice not revealing any of the horror the big man had for going into the street.

"No, I can handle it myself, Earl, but what I want you to do while I'm gone is stay on this thing dealing with Janet. If you find out where she's at, don't make any moves. I'll call you when I get to Los Angeles and let you know where I'm staying. So all I really want you to do is be my ears while I'm gone."

"You want I should take care of the pimp?" Earl asked.

For a second, Daddy Cool hesitated, thinking the request over. It would be a good time to take the young pimp out of it. Being out of town was the best alibi in the world. That way nobody could put the deed at his doorstep.

"I don't know, Earl. I had better wait awhile and find out just how much Ronald is involved with Janet. I'd hate to do something to the kid, then find out he really didn't have her stashed away somewhere," Daddy Cool stated, after slow deliberation. The idea had been such a good one that he was really tempted. It was a wonderful opportunity to get the young pimp out of his hair once and for all.

Earl, listening closely, could tell his friend was undecided. "It won't be no trouble, Larry. Just give me the go-ahead sign and I'll take care of it for you."

Daddy Cool laughed. "Don't be in such a hurry, Earl. All in good time, brother, all in good time." But even as Daddy Cool made the statement, the image of the young pimp flashed across his mind, and for a brief second he was like some frenzied beast who had caught the scent of his prey. It was hard for him to tolerate the thought of his young daughter laying up at nights with the boy. Assassination was really the simplest solution to his problem.

Before he weakened and gave Earl an order he might come to regret, Daddy Cool hung up the receiver. He stared down at the telephone while his subconscious mind ran wild, picturing bedroom scenes that it would have been best not to think about.

Invariably his thoughts came back around to the decision he had made about taking the contract. He debated with himself on the merits of that. Common sense told him that it was too much money to pass up for any flimsy reason. Janet had made her bed, so she would just have to lie in it. Concentrating on the upcoming job, he was finally able to put the brooding thoughts of Janet out of his mind.

When the telephone in his bedroom began to ring, Daddy Cool walked hurriedly to answer. He picked up the receiver.

"Okay, Al," he said quickly, "I'll take ten grand now and the other fifteen when the job's finished."

"Good, good," came the voice from the other end of the line. "You can come on over now and get your money. While you're here, I'll brief you on what you'll have to know. We got the punk's address and everything, so all you need to do is get there and handle it in your same old manner."

Daddy Cool hung up the telephone, then called out to his wife. "Shirley, I want you to pack me a few things. I'm going to take a trip to the West Coast," he stated, as his wife came hurrying into the bedroom.

"While I'm gone, Shirley, if you hear from Janet, tell her I'm sorry and ask her to come back home. Tell her I said I'll buy her a small compact car just for her if she's here when I get back."

Shirley wasn't surprised by her husband's instant generosity. It was his way whenever he tried to make up for something he had done. Money or gifts were always the result. He believed he could pay for anything.

Daddy Cool walked over to his closet and pulled out a heavy strongbox. He took a key from his pocket and opened the huge lock on it. Opening the dresser drawer, he removed the ten thousand dollars he had so carelessly thrown inside the dresser. Shirley watched him silently.

Again there was no surprise. She had long ago become accustomed to seeing him with extremely large sums of money. Yet she had no idea where it came from. But over the years she had started putting small things together. Whenever he came back from a trip, he always seemed to have large sums of cash.

After asking once about it and getting cursed out for being too damn nosey, she didn't make that mistake again. Her man was a cold one, and she had long ago found out that she was out of her element when dealing with him.

Now that he had finally made up his mind, Daddy Cool felt better about the whole thing. Maybe this was what he needed: a trip, so that he could get his mind off his family problems. He began to dress with care as he wondered idly about which technique he would use on this contract. Well, he reasoned, the best thing to do was wait until he knew more about it, then he could decide on how best to handle it.

One thing was sure though: there wouldn't be any gun used. No, not this time. No way was he going to try and take a gun on an airplane. His best bet would be to just wait until he got to California; then he would see how the case needed handling.

For now, the best thing for him to do would be to hurry on over and pick up the ten grand. Yeah, the thought of the money brought a smile to his cold, expressionless face.

6

A S THE WARNING LIGHT came on in the airplane, Daddy Cool felt the old uneasiness that always filled him whenever his plane landed or took off. He quickly fastened his seatbelt, then put out the cigarette he had been smoking. It had been a fast trip anyway, he reasoned. He glanced out the window beside him and saw the lights of Los Angeles down below.

To take his mind off the landing, he removed the picture of the man he was seeking and stared at it closely. He would know the face now if he met the man in a crowd. On and off for the past six hours he had been reading the file he had on the man.

The envelope containing the file was still in his lap, though he had orders to destroy it as soon as he was acquainted with everything inside of the small dossier. It told in detail of the man's habits. Every little quirk of the man was written down inside the folder.

Suddenly the airplane bounced once, then landed smoothly. They taxied down the runway swiftly. Daddy Cool had that indescribable feeling in the pit of his stomach as the airplane began to slow down. He wiped the sweat off his face and began to take off his safety belt. The stewardess came down the aisle and gave him a bright smile, then asked if he had a pleasant trip.

"Yes," he replied, "I had an enjoyable trip, thank you."

He spoke softly, then watched her walk on down the aisle. Now that the plane was coming to a halt, all his earlier apprehensions disappeared. I guess I'll never get used to flying, Daddy Cool told himself.

The tall, elderly white woman across from him smiled in his direction when she saw him look up and catch her eye. She had been eyeing the attractive black man ever since she had boarded the airplane, and while on the trip west she had cursed herself for not having the nerve to have taken the seat next to him. It wasn't every day that she had a chance to meet a man that attractive. Now, as she watched him stand up and get ready to leave the plane, she realized someone she would have loved knowing was getting ready to walk out of her life.

"I say, sir," she said hesitatingly, "would you help me get my small handbag down, please?"

Daddy Cool glanced coldly at the woman. He had noticed the glances she had been casting his way all during the trip but had pointedly ignored them. The last thing he wanted was to get involved with a woman. That was one of his rules whenever he was on a job. He never became involved with a woman.

But helping her get her bag wouldn't be an involvement, so he quickly reached up and removed the bag she had pointed out. It was very light, and he knew at once that she could have handled it with ease. Since she was tall, she wouldn't have had any problem. Before he had only a hunch that she wanted some action, but now he knew it was a fact.

Without seeming to be rude, he gave her the bag, then quickly mumbled something that she couldn't understand and made his escape down the aisle. The woman followed slowly, surprised at the handsome man's action. He actually seemed to be in a hurry to get away from her. Maybe his wife was waiting for him, she decided, and slowed her pace down even more. The last thing she needed was a scene with some angry woman.

Daddy Cool was one of the first people out of the airplane. He hurried down the ramp and quickly disappeared inside the terminal. With his long strides he quickly crossed the waiting room and went out the door. He waved down the first cab he saw and gave an address in Hollywood.

Daddy Cool settled back and enjoyed the scenery as the cab moved swiftly through the traffic on Imperial Street. The driver reached the freeway and turned onto it. Soon they were moving swiftly in the evening traffic on the freeway.

It seemed as if he had just gotten comfortable when the cab pulled off the freeway and turned right on Wilshire Boulevard. In another minute the cab pulled up in front of an old hotel.

Daddy Cool removed his one bag and paid the cab fare. He walked slowly into the dimly lit building. The hotel had seen better days, that he was sure of. If his prey hadn't been staying at the Gilbert Hotel, Daddy Cool would never have chosen it for his lodgings. He checked in under a false name and paid his rent for two weeks. That way, he reasoned, the people on the desk wouldn't have any cause to disturb him for anything.

After putting his suitcase away, he walked down the hall until he found the incinerator. Quickly he pushed the folder down inside it and waited to make sure it had fallen down the chute. He made his way back to his room and stretched out on the bed. After taking another glance at his watch, he decided to turn in. There was a four-hour time difference from Michigan, so it was still fairly early.

Just ten o'clock in the evening. But Daddy Cool felt tired. Before turning in, he took a quick shower and cursed when he found out he didn't have any hot water. Rubbing himself vigorously, he climbed in between the sheets and soon was fast asleep.

When the first rays of the morning sunlight came through his window, Daddy Cool climbed out of the bed. He felt refreshed now and decided that he would get right on the case. He took a shower, then opened his suitcase and dressed in dark work pants. The shirt he put on was black with long sleeves.

Now that he looked more like a working man, he decided he was ready. He stopped in the hotel lobby and set his watch by the clock downstairs. It was just nine o'clock in the morning, but early enough for people to be up and around.

He wished there was some way he could check to find out if his hiding contract man was still in the hotel. Daddy Cool had the number of the informant who had sold them the information in the first place, but he didn't want to contact the man. The less he had to do with strangers the better off he would be.

He crossed the dingy hotel lobby, studying the faces of the few occupants of the hotel who were already up and sipping coffee from a machine and gossiping with each other. He noticed that most of them were elderly people who had more than likely stayed at this hotel for years. The women looked to be in their fifties, while the two men he saw were just as old.

Once outside he walked slowly down the street until he found a restaurant that appeared to be fairly clean. He found a seat near the front window and ordered pancakes with a large glass of milk. After eating, Daddy Cool caught a cab and rode up to Hollywood Boulevard, where he got out and, beginning at one end of the block, slowly took his time and searched for the small store he was looking for.

In the third block he finally found it. He went in and examined the knives on display in the case. He had the woman pull out two long-bladed hunting knives. These he went over closely. After a long, careful examination, he walked back out without buying anything. He stood outside the store and searched the display windows until he found the knives he had examined in the window display.

After that, he took his time and walked around. It was later in the day when he found just what he was looking for. A tall, slim black man approached him and asked for a quarter.

"What you want, brother, some wine money?" Daddy Cool inquired, staring coldly at the man.

The winehead hesitated for a second. Before he could frame his lie, Daddy Cool spoke up again. "I was gettin' ready to buy me a taste, but if you don't want any, that's cool with me."

The man wiped his lips with the back of his hand. The shirt he had on was filthy. Dirt was everywhere. Daddy Cool led the man to the nearest store, then went in and bought a bottle. They walked around until they found an alley. There Daddy Cool knocked the top off the bottle and took a long drink. When he finished, he passed the bottle to his friend, who had been watching him drink with watery eyes.

"How would you like to make five dollars?" Daddy Cool inquired as the man drained the bottle.

"What I got to do, bro," the man asked in a hoarse, whiskey-filled voice.

"I was going to buy two huntin' knives so that when I went fishing I could use them to clean my fish. But I got to arguing with the woman in the store and now I'm ashamed to go back inside and buy them myself. I told her I could get them down the street cheaper, but the motherfuckers cost more down the street," Daddy Cool stated, watching the man's reactions out of the corner of his eye.

"Now, I'll give you five dollars to go in the store and get them for me, but I don't want you comin' out with the wrong thing, nigger."

"You ain't got to worry 'bout no shit like that happenin'," the man stated.

"Good, then," Daddy Cool replied, then began to lead the way back to the store. He stopped in front of the display window. "I don't want that white bitch in there to see me, man. Those are the knives I want."

The drunk stared fish-eyed at him. "Man, you sure that's all you want me to do?"

"I just want you to do that, and that's all, man. But like I said, I don't want no shit out of you. I know how much they cost, and I'm going to give you the right money, so don't go in there and buy the wrong thing. If you do you ain't goin' get no five dollars."

Daddy Cool pointed out the knives again. "You notice the white bone handle on the end, well, they ain't got no other kind in there, so you shouldn't make no mistake."

"I ain't goin' make no mistake, man," the drunk replied, still suspicious.

Daddy Cool counted the money out in the drunk's hand, then held back five dollars. "Now, this is yours whenever you come out with the right knives. You dig?"

The drunk took the money, nodding his head. Daddy Cool watched him stagger off into the store. He smiled as he realized that the white saleswoman would be scared shitless at the sight of the bum. But it was better this way, he reasoned. If the knives were ever traced, she would remember the funky drunk while forgetting about the customer earlier who hadn't bought either knife.

In a few minutes the drunk came out, clutching a bag to his chest. He looked back in the store and cursed. "I see what you mean, my man," he said as he came up to Daddy Cool. "That stupid bitch wouldn't even pull the motherfuckin' knives out until after I showed her some money. I mean," the man continued, "people just don't do business that way, you understand what I mean?"

Slowly disengaging the man's hand from the bag that contained the knives, Daddy Cool agreed with him. Keeping up a steady flow of bullshit with the man, he checked the package, making sure it had just what he wanted.

"Here you go, old man," Daddy Cool stated as he removed an old bill from his pocket. He shoved the five-dollar bill into the drunk's hand.

"Next time I need a good man," Daddy Cool stated slowly,

53

"I'm goin' be sure to look you up, my man," he said as he began to walk in the opposite direction of the bum.

The bum waved his hand in farewell. He was only too glad to see the man he considered a fool leave. All the time Daddy Cool had been talking, the bum had been afraid that the man would change his mind and try to keep the five dollars. Now that he had the money clutched tightly in his fist, he hurried away, wanting to put as much distance between him and the giver as possible.

Daddy Cool grinned as he watched the bum hurrying away. Without another backward glance, Daddy Cool made his way to the nearest main street and hailed a cab for the short trip back to his hotel.

He went immediately up to his room and relaxed. After taking a quick shower, Daddy Cool removed the two knives from the bag. He began practicing with them until he was well acquainted with each one. After an hour of steady knife throwing, he knew he could hit his target without any trouble. He now handled the two knives as if they had been in his hands since birth.

Moving with slow deliberation, Daddy Cool removed the picture of the man he was tracing from his coat and studied it closely. When he finished, he replaced the picture. After dressing in an old dark-blue suit that was at least ten years old, Daddy Cool placed a man's wig on his head. The wig was a bushy natural. He studied the effects of his appearance in the mirror.

Not quite satisfied, he took out a jar and opened it. He began applying the lotion from the jar onto the palms of his hands, then slowly rubbed it evenly over his face. After about ten minutes, he replaced the lid. The effect of the lotion was instantly recognizable.

His skin color had changed slightly. Now he appeared to be much darker than normal. The tanning process had worked quickly. Instead of there being a light-skinned black man, now there was a brown-complexioned man staring back at him out of the old dresser mirror. Taking his time, Daddy Cool went into the toilet and washed his hands, making sure there were no traces of the mixture he had used.

Daddy Cool took one more look at himself in the mirror before leaving. After that, he let himself out into the hallway. Daddy Cool walked down the stairway and made his way into the lobby. He bought a cup of coffee out of the machine, then found a soft cushioned chair and sat down. He picked up an old newspaper lying on the table and hid his face behind it. The seat he took allowed him to see everybody who came in and out of the hotel door.

He was visible only to the people who walked in the area on the right side of the desk. True, anyone taking the stairway up or down would be able to see him clearly, but for the people coming in and going up to the desk, he would only be an outline.

For the next two days Daddy Cool continued to keep his close watch on the lobby. On the morning of the third day he broke luck. The man he had been waiting for walked through the entrance of the hotel carrying an overnight bag.

It dawned on Daddy Cool at once that his prey was just returning to the hotel from some trip. For the past days the man hadn't been living at the hotel. The key to the man's room was behind the desk on a peg, which Daddy Cool had noticed before. Now the desk clerk took the key down and pushed it under the bulletproof glass that separated the clerk from his customers.

From out of the corner of his eye, Daddy Cool watched the man take the key and head for the elevator. The man looked around the lobby nervously before the elevator arrived and he stepped inside the cubicle. From his movements Daddy Cool knew that the man was nervous. That much, at least, was obvious to anybody.

As the door closed behind the man and the elevator started up, Daddy Cool began to put his plan together. It had been impossible for him to make any complete plans earlier because he hadn't been sure that the man was still staying at the hotel. Now that he was sure, he could get the job over and done with. And the sooner the better.

He quickly dismissed the idea of just knocking on the man's door and making the hit on him when he opened it. Anything could go wrong with the hit if he tried it that way. The man might come to the door with a pistol in his hand or somebody could step out of an apartment just when he got ready to knock the sucker off.

No, it would have to be done in a different way. But how? The question leaped through his mind. How? How? How? Ruthlessly he dismissed one idea after another until he thought his head would burst.

The last thing he wanted to do was expose himself to danger. It would have to be done smoothly. There could be no mistake.

On the third day of his constant watch, Daddy Cool decided that something would have to be done to bring things to a head. He was tired of sitting in the lobby with the old people who made up most of the customers in the hotel. Walking over to the coffee machine, Daddy Cool bought his fourth cup of coffee, then walked back to his seat and sat down.

If only, Daddy Cool reflected, the bastard would leave his room at night. He had waited and hoped that he could catch his prey out in the streets somewhere, but the man never went out at night. Daddy Cool glanced at his watch. It was almost one o'clock in the morning. The midnight clerk had come on duty.

Daddy Cool had just about made up his mind to turn in for the night when suddenly the man he stalked came hurrying out of the elevator. The man glanced right and left as he walked swiftly across the lobby. Daddy Cool waited until the doors had closed behind the hurrying figure, then he got up and began following him.

Daddy Cool was just in time to see his man get into a cab. He glanced up and down the nearly deserted street, cursing under his breath as his keen eyes saw the empty street. He cursed harshly as he realized that it was his own fault. He hadn't bothered to rent a car since he had believed he would end up making the hit inside the hotel.

Suddenly Daddy Cool saw bright headlights swing onto the boulevard from one of the smaller side streets. Quickly he stepped out into the street from the curb. He raised his hands in the air and began to wave wildly, all the time trying to keep the car in front of him in his eyesight.

The cab driver started to stop. But it seemed as though, as soon as the driver saw that it was a black man trying to wave him down, he pressed down on the gas pedal and the cab leaped forward.

"You cocksucker," Daddy Cool yelled after the disappearing cab.

He turned on his heels and retraced his steps back toward the entrance of the hotel. More angry at himself than he was with the cab driver, Daddy Cool stopped in front of the hotel. It was too hot, he reasoned, to be shut up in the tiny hotel room. Even though there was a slight breeze blowing, the night air seemed to be choking him.

As he started to walk around the block his mind returned to the subject that constantly stayed with him—his wayward daughter. If only he could keep her off his mind he would be able to take care of the job he was sent out to do. So far, all he could do was reflect on the mistakes he had made since arriving on the West Coast.

Altogether, he had made too many errors. In his line of work, mistakes were very costly. At the rate he was going, he reflected, he would end up paying the dues he owed, too. For the obvious reason, he just couldn't bring his full concentration to the job at hand. Janet. Janet would be his damn downfall if he didn't change his ways.

He couldn't help but wonder if there had been any changes in the young girl's mind since she had left. Enough time had passed. She had been gone long enough to forgive her father for what he had done in the heat of his anger. There was no reason for her still to hold a grudge against him, yet he realized that was what was wrong. Her temper, just like his own, was her worst enemy. When angry, she didn't take time to think anything out; she just reacted.

As he continued to walk, deep in his moody thoughts, he failed to notice the group of six young boys who turned around and started to follow him on the narrow side street. The darkness of the street suited his black mood. The six boys crossed over so that they were now about fifty feet behind him. Their steps picked up as they started to gain on the tall black man in front of them.

Any other time, Daddy Cool would have recognized the danger he was walking into. But now, with his mind three thousand miles away, he never even glanced up when the loud sounds of hurrying footsteps should have warned him of approaching danger.

The first warning he had was when someone tapped him on the shoulder. He glanced around without really thinking of what he was doing.

"What the hell," Daddy Cool managed to say; then his keen nerves sent warning signs that almost exploded in his head. You fool, he cursed himself. What the hell have you allowed yourself to walk into? The question inside his mind was never answered. Before he could figure out some kind of defense, another hand touched him on the other shoulder.

Daddy Cool was a product of the ghetto streets, so by nature he knew what a trick would run into. Yet he had allowed himself to fall into the very same trap that tricks ran into every day when they slummed in the black neighborhood after dark. It was even possible that the young group of boys had mistaken him for a white man in the dark. Whatever the reason, only swift action would save him now. Even though the gang now realized that it wasn't a white man they had stopped, they were too far committed to back off now. Whatever the result, they would play it to the end.

Knowing that swift action was the only thing that would save him, Daddy Cool still hesitated a second too long. When he did make his move, he was seconds too late. One of the boys had his arm pinned behind his back, while another large black boy slammed him twice in the stomach. The vicious punches brought a gasp of pain from their victim. Daddy Cool bent double from the blow. Another fist struck him behind the neck.

Daddy Cool felt like a fool. The beating he was taking was all because of his stupidity. If he had kept his mind open and alert, none of this would be happening. Suddenly he felt a hand feeling around in his back pocket. He wanted to scream out for them to take it, just take the money and leave him alone. He knew that there was only about two hundred dollars in the wallet, plus some funny identification. He wouldn't miss the money or the ID. He only prayed that his attackers wouldn't hurt him too badly.

So instead of trying to resist, he played possum. He went limp in the hands that held him up, allowing the hoodlums to do what they would, trying to show them that he wasn't going to give them any trouble. To fight back would only bring down worse punishment on him. Since he couldn't reach the knives he carried strapped to his back, there wasn't too much he could do with just his hands.

"I got it!" a young excited voice called out.

"Make sure, goddamn it," a huskier voice answered. "Remember last time, ya ran off with the fuckin' wallet and wasn't nothin' in it."

"Shit," the excited voice came again, "this bastard was loaded. It's full of big bills."

Daddy Cool was thankful that they had found the money. Now, with luck, they would run off and leave him alone. But even as the fleeting thought ran across his mind, he was struck viciously against the side of his head. A moan escaped from him, and the pain reached him with a jar. He realized now that the young hoodlums might just decide to kill him in case he had recognized one of them.

He grabbed his head and tried to fall to the ground. Strong arms still held him tightly, so he managed only to wiggle around in their grasp. Instantly, blows began to rain on him from all sides. Again he tried to break the grip that held him. Fear gave him strength so that he finally got one arm free.

"Goddamn it," he cursed loudly, "take the money, you bastards, and go!" He screamed loudly, his voice rose to a pitch that he couldn't recognize.

For his troubles, he received a blow in the mouth that he knew cut his lips. He could taste the fresh blood running from the cut.

"Not yet, you motherfucker," a harsh voice stated.

Then all the pain in the world burst loose in his nuts as one of his attackers kicked him viciously between the legs.

Without warning, the pavement came up and struck him in the face. He lay stretched out on the cold ground as he heard the footsteps running away in the dark. He knew he should be thankful, but the pain he was feeling was too great. He couldn't understand what he should be thankful for. It seemed like hours, but it had only been seconds, when he heard a woman's voice speaking to him. It sounded as if she was a long way away.

"Are you all right, mister? We saw them boys attacking you from our car and waited until they let you go before we got out." The woman seemed to be waiting for an answer; then she spoke to the other person with her.

"Sally, maybe we should call the police. He seems to be hurt real bad."

"You want me to drive up and find a pay phone somewhere?" Sally asked.

For a second the other woman hesitated, then spoke sharply. There was fear in her voice. "No way, honey, you ain't 'bout to leave me standing out here in the dark. Shit, them niggers might come back!"

At the mention of the police, Daddy Cool's mind began to work. He knew he couldn't stand any police questions. There was even the chance they might search him and, when they found the knives he carried, he would be in a world of trouble.

"No police," he managed to say. "Please, just help me to my feet," he begged the woman nearest to him.

As she began to lift him up, he tried to help her, but the pain was too great. He let out a loud moan.

"Damn, honey," the woman lifting him said, "you're hurt real bad, man. Maybe you better go to the hospital and let them look at you."

From somewhere, Daddy Cool found the strength to stand up. He managed to stand on his own feet, with the woman's helpful arms around him. "I'll be okay," he mumbled. "If I can get back to my home, I'll be able to handle it from there."

The woman stared at him curiously. "Well, it's your own business, but if it was me, I'd sure as hell go to the hospital and let them have a look at me."

Daddy Cool knew the woman was right, but he couldn't stand being undressed at the hospital, not as long as he carried the brace of knives strapped to his back. Maybe after stashing the weapons in his room he could then take the risk of going and getting medical help, but not until after he had cleaned up.

He tried to stand without the help of the woman. There was a sharp pain in his ribs, but other than that he felt as if he was all right. First he tried to take two short steps. The pain was sharp, yet he believed it was possible for him to walk. If only he didn't have to walk all the way back to his hotel.

"Miss," he began, "if you would be kind enough to drop me off at my home, I'd gladly pay you for your troubles."

The heavyset black woman glanced at him curiously. She seemed as though she would say no, so he spoke up hurriedly. "It's only a couple of blocks away, miss, and I'd gladly pay you for any trouble it would cause you."

Before she could answer, her friend spoke up. "We might as well, girl; he can't hardly give us any trouble when he can't even walk."

The woman helping Daddy Cool glanced over at her friend. "Okay," she finally said. "I guess we can do that much for you." Between the two women, they helped him to the car.

When he bent down to get into the car, pain exploded inside of him. For one brief moment, Daddy Cool thought he would pass out. Gradually the pain became bearable. He gritted his teeth and fought back the tendency to faint. He was glad to see the hotel, after directing the women to it. At first, he had wanted to give them the wrong address and get out near the hotel, but the pain was too harsh. He didn't believe he had the strength to make it without their help.

"You should go to the hospital," the woman called Sally stated sharply.

Daddy Cool tried to smile. "I would go, but I don't even know where a hospital is at, and," he continued, not giving the woman time to speak, "I don't even have enough money left on me to catch a cab back. After I go up to my room and get some money, I'll take your advice and seek out a hospital."

After the woman driving parked in front of the hotel, Sally, sitting on the driver's side, climbed out and held the door open for him.

"You see," she said as he tried to get out without her help, "you can't even stand up by yourself."

This time Daddy Cool didn't attempt to smile. The pain was too great.

"I must go up to my room and get some money," he finally managed to say. "If you ladies would be kind enough to wait and take me to the hospital, I'd be willing to pay you for your troubles. But I must get some money," he stated. "It wouldn't make sense coming out of the hospital and havin' to catch a bus."

The driver began to shake her head.

"I don't know if we'll have that much time," she stated, staring past Daddy Cool and catching her friend's eye.

"Aw shit, Doris," Sally said, "it won't take that much time to just drop him off at General Hospital. You can see he ain't in no shape to help himself."

Before Doris could answer, Daddy Cool added, "I'll give you ten dollars for your trouble, miss."

The driver hesitated, then said quickly, "Okay, if you don't spend too long up in your room, 'cause I've got to be gettin' on."

"You want me to help you?" Sally inquired, when she saw the trouble he was having trying to stay on his feet. Daddy Cool could only nod his head. The woman put her arm around him and started for the door. Before they reached the entrance, Doris joined them. Between the two women, they managed to get him up the steps of the hotel.

The desk clerk glanced sharply at the threesome as they came into the hotel. Daddy Cool didn't have to go to the desk for his key since he made it a habit to carry it on him at all times. They took the elevator upstairs, while the few people still up stared after them curiously.

Once upstairs, Daddy Cool managed to open his door. Again, the women stayed right with him as he went into the small bedroom.

The only way he could get some privacy was to excuse himself and stumble into the tiny bathroom. Once inside with the door closed, Daddy Cool had to fight back the weakness that constantly tried to overcome him. He finally was able to take off his coat, then remove his shirt. For a second, he thought he might have to ask one of the women to come in and help him take off the harness that held his knives.

But with the strength of desperation, he struggled with the catch until he was able to take it off himself. Sweat rolled off his forehead from the incredible pain that racked his body from the struggle to remove the weapons. He let out a sigh of relief.

"Are you all right?" Sally called out.

"Yes," he managed to reply. Picking up his shirt he carried it over his arm as he opened the door. One backward glance assured him that the knives hidden under the bathtub couldn't be seen from the doorway.

Both women stared at him closely as he came out. He walked over to the closet to remove one of the suitcases, but it hurt too bad for him to bend over.

"Please," he pleaded, as he kicked at the suitcase that he wanted.

Sally saw what he wanted, picked up the suitcase for him, and carried it over to the bed.

"Open it, please," he asked, standing beside the bed between the women.

With a shake of her head, Sally quickly obeyed his request. For a second, Daddy Cool hesitated to reveal so much money to the women, but he knew he didn't have any other choice. As soon as she opened the buckles, he flipped back the lid. Most of his money was hidden under some white shirts, so all he had to do was slip his hand under the clothes and remove one of the bundles.

The small bundle of money he pulled out still was wrapped in the white money wrapper. The sum on the wrapper read five hundred dollars. The top bills were brand new one-hundred-dollar bills. He flipped the top bills back and extracted a twenty-dollar bill.

Taking it loose from the rest, he held it out to Doris, then removed another twenty-dollar bill and gave it to Sally. Both women tried not to accept the money, but Daddy Cool could tell they wanted it. He wouldn't listen to their denials; he just pushed the money into their hands.

"Listen," he stated, "I need help, and the best way to get it is to pay for it. I know both of you have something else to do, but if I pay you for your trouble, maybe it won't be too difficult for you to put off whatever you were going to do."

Before they could say anything, he added, "Once we get to the hospital, you can go your own way, but if ya should stay with me, I'll give both of you another twenty when we leave. How does that sound?" He saw the greed in their eyes as he mentioned money.

"Well," Doris began, "whatever I had to do, I sure as hell wasn't going to make forty dollars at it, so I got the time now."

Sally seemed to be ashamed. She stared down at the floor. "It seems funny to accept money for helping somebody, but my kids can sure use the cash."

"Well then, it's settled, huh?" Daddy Cool managed a slight smile as each of the women moved to one side of him to help.

Daddy Cool reflected on the merits of money as Doris drove swiftly to the nearest hospital. Since giving the women the money, he couldn't help but notice the change in them. Money made people function better, or so it seemed. Though he had their help without paying them, they seemed even more helpful after he gave them money.

He knew he had taken a chance letting them see his money, but since one of them had on a nurse's uniform, he didn't think he had too much to fear from them. They were just hardworking black women. Even if the thought of robbing him had passed through their minds, they were not of the caliber of robbers. It was something he could sense.

At the hospital, the two women waited patiently while doctors bandaged up Daddy Cool's ribs. He walked out slowly and informed the women that he had two broken ribs. On the ride back to his hotel, he had them stop so he could buy them both a dinner, ordering his to be taken out.

With the hot food in his lap and his ribs wrapped up, he realized that the situation he had fallen into could have turned out a whole lot worse if it hadn't been for the help of the two black women.

He felt a deep gratitude for their help and a slow anger at himself for allowing his mind to linger on his silly daughter to such a degree that he walked into a trap that any child in the ghetto would have avoided.

At the hotel he thanked the women, then removed a hundred-dollar bill from his bankroll. They tried to turn it down, but he knew they wanted it. After giving them the money, he said, "Well, sisters, I've seen enough of California. I think I'll catch the morning plane back to New York."

Daddy Cool removed a pencil from his pocket and wrote out a fake address. "If either of you are ever in New York, just call me at this address and I'll show you the town. Take care now, and be sure you don't walk into any muggers." He flashed his smile at the women before turning on his heel and limping slowly toward the hotel door.

7

AT THE SAME MOMENT that Daddy Cool walked back into his hotel room, his daughter, Janet, was just awakening back in the Motor City. She stared around the small, dirty apartment her boyfriend had found for her. It was cheaper than the motel and had roaches.

After finishing her morning toilet, she made her daily telephone call to her mother. Since her father had left on another one of his unexplainable trips, she had gotten into the habit of talking with her mother on the phone every morning. It allowed her mind to relax. She could think back on how nice it used to be.

At times like this, she wished with all her heart she was back home with no problems. Whenever something came up she couldn't handle, all she had to do was wait for her father and explain it to him. He could handle anything.

Janet bit her lip. For a second she thought she was going to start crying again. That wouldn't do at all. Lately, she had found herself bursting into tears for no reason. Ronald had called her a "spoiled crybaby" and walked out on her two days ago, and she hadn't heard from him since. Now she wondered if he was ever going to come back. She knew she had acted like a child, getting mad over the other women he had.

Ronald had come out and told her point-blank that he wasn't about to fire his whores and get a job just to take care of her. Remembering the argument started the tears to flowing again. She sat in front of her tiny cracked mirror and watched the tears running down her cheeks. She wished with all her heart she had known that was the way he had felt before she had gone to bed with him.

Now she felt like something dirty. The sex had been all right, but she could have done without it. Now, no longer a virgin, she was beginning to grow up, and she didn't like the way it felt. Making up her mind on different problems was almost too much for her. She wasn't used to it and wished with all her heart she had a man like her father to take care of everything.

After about ten minutes of self-pity, Janet got control of herself and held back the rest of the tears. Crying didn't do any good. The same problems were still there after crying her heart out. The only thing she ever accomplished was to smear her makeup.

Finally Janet managed to pull herself together. After taking a shower, she dressed carefully, wanting to look her best when Ronald arrived. She pulled on a short black slip, then slipped into a tight-fitting dark-green skirt with matching jacket.

The miniskirt was exceedingly short, revealing her beautiful legs, while the white sweater she wore under the green jacket revealed nicely her well-developed chest. By the time she was fully dressed, it was past the time Ronald had said he would arrive.

Again she was disturbed by doubts and fears. If Ronald didn't show up, she believed she would go out of her mind. Since she was so disturbed, she began pulling out the dresser drawers, searching for the pint of whiskey Ronald had left there the night he stayed.

She had just found the strong drink and poured herself a stiff one when she heard him knock on the door. At once she knew who it was because nobody else knocked with their car keys except him.

Hurriedly she turned the glass up and downed the fierce burning alcohol in one swallow. The whiskey almost took her breath away. She had never taken over three drinks in her life. Now, before she could go to the door, she had to fight back the tears that the drink brought to her eyes. Once again, the sound of knocking came to her and she staggered over to the door, gaining control with each second.

"Hi, honey," she managed to say as she greeted him at the door.

Ronald, rather short in size, was a dark-complexioned man who wore the new-style high-heel shoes. The black-and-white shoes he wore matched an expensive checkered sport coat with black pants that had huge flaring cuffs.

When she tried to kiss him, Ronald turned his cheek so that she could only peck him on the side of the face. His sharp, piercing black eyes took in the whiskey bottle sitting on top of the dresser. His eyebrows went up as he held her at arms length.

"Well, when the hell did this shit begin," he inquired, nodding at the bottle.

"Oh," she said, blushing, "I just felt like taking a taste, Ron, that's all."

Before he could answer, she continued. "You know I don't really drink, so why are you concerned?"

He shrugged his shoulders, then stated, "From the way your breath smells, you sure in the hell would have trouble trying to explain you didn't drink to a policeman, if one should stop us and smelled your breath. Now get your ass in the bathroom and wash your mouth out. I want you to kill that fuckin' odor. Where I'm gettin' ready to take you, I don't want the people to think I brought a juice-head along with me."

Blushing, Janet hurried into the bathroom to obey his orders.

Quickly she brushed her teeth, then rinsed out her mouth. When she felt sure that there was no more odor about her, she returned. Stopping in front of him, she again tried to embrace her man.

Ronald took her arms from around his neck. "We ain't got time for all that shit," he stated, then added, "Besides, I just had my hair done and I don't want it to get messed up." Even as he spoke, he raised his hand and patted the old-fashioned process. His hair gleamed like shiny black gold from the barber's oil.

Janet took the rebuke and let her hands drop back to her sides. For some reason she felt she was getting on Ronald's nerves. It hadn't been like this until after she had left home. Before, it seemed to her he couldn't keep his hands off of her. Now it was the other way around. She couldn't believe he was tired of her already, but it sure as hell seemed like it.

Maybe it was because of the hunt her father was staging. Everybody knew he had put out some kind of reward for information concerning her whereabouts. But when they had first heard about it, Ronald had only laughed. Now, for some reason, it wasn't funny to him any longer. He seemed to brood over it.

"Honey . . . ," she began, but he cut her off quickly.

"Goddamn it, Janet, how many times have I got to tell you to stop calling me 'honey' all the time. It's just as bad as being called 'sweetie.' It's a term whores use when they talk to their tricks. Can't you get that through your head?"

She shook her head dumbfoundedly. "I didn't know, hon, I mean, Ronald. But I don't see why it should upset you. I'm not a whore, so why let a word disturb you?"

Ronald tossed his hands in the air, making a gesture. "Shit, woman, it don't make a damn if you're a whore or not. It's just my bad luck that you're not one. Shit, that's all I'd need, a young fine bitch with enough sense to get the money, but no, I couldn't be that lucky. Hell no, I got to have a square bitch that ain't got enough sense to get fifty cents, let alone a few hundred."

His words beat at her, ringing in her ears. She could hardly believe what she had heard. Spurred on by her inner conflict, she wanted to hear more. It was time for them to lay their cards on the table. Even though there was a savage pain inside of her, she drove herself ruthlessly until she heard the question coming out of her mouth. It was as if someone else was talking and she was just an innocent bystander, watching and listening.

"You mean," she said softly, "that you would rather see me out in the streets selling my body than for me to be here trying to make a nice cozy home for us?" She held her breath, waiting for his answer.

Ronald stared at her coldly. He knew he had let the cat out of the bag too soon. He had meant to play it slow, until the day came when he was sure she would be ready. Now it would have to be done another way. But again, caution was needed. She was too young and inexperienced to rush things at her, so he would have to be devious if he hoped to turn her out.

"Baby," he began and opened his arms to take her into them. He slowly stroked her back as he talked quietly into her ear. "I don't want to sound rough, Janet, but it's just that I've got a lot on my mind. The finance people are worrying the fuck out of me because I'm out of ready cash. Here I am two car notes behind and it's worrying the shit out of me. You know, Janet, I don't want to lose my car, so it's worryin' me. Maybe that's why I seem short with you, you dig?" He held her back and stared into her eyes. Even with the high-heeled shoes he wore, he was still an inch shorter than she was.

Janet tried to shake her head and knew she was going to cry. "I didn't know, Ronald, I swear; I didn't have the slightest idea you were uptight like that."

"Yeah, baby, I know. I didn't want to worry you with my petty-ass problems, so I didn't mention it to you. But I've been hidin' my car at nights so that they won't repossess it. But goddamn, Janet, you should have dug something. If my cash had been right, do you think I would have stuck you in this motherfuckin' pigpen? Shit, baby, I sure think more of you than to want to see you living in something like this. It's just that I don't have the bread right now to do it better. Once I catch up, everything is going to be all right."

Her brain was whirling beneath the stunning revelation. If he couldn't pay for his car, how the hell did she expect him to be able to take care of her? Again the thought flashed across her mind about him getting a job, but she didn't know how to approach him with it.

At least she could be thankful that she hadn't broken down and cried on him. That wouldn't have helped, and he would have thought her a child instead of a young lady.

Ronald, on the other hand, was reading her like a book. He saw the tears in the corner of her eyes and silently cursed. There was another way, he reasoned quickly, and even while the thought ran briefly through his mind, he bent his head and kissed her on the neck.

His breath was hot on the curve of her neck as he brought all his experience of lovemaking into play. From her neck he went down slowly, pushing the blouse down. Finding it in his way, he pushed her back toward the bed, gently laying her down. With the professional care of a man who knew what he was doing, he slowly began to undress her. First, he removed the dark-green jacket she wore. Next he opened the distance between them so that he could get the blouse she wore off.

Even as he slowly undressed her, he continuously placed passionate kisses on her exposed body. As soon as he had her blouse off, he began to kiss each tit with slow, endearing kisses. He dragged it out until she began to pant like a dog in heat. Her breathing became ragged as her desire began to build to a pitch she couldn't control.

The sex they had before was nothing like what she was now experiencing. Her nerves tingled. Everywhere he touched was like a hot burning fire placed on her skin. She moaned in her aroused condition. Yet it was not enough. Ronald continued to play with her.

He took her skirt off, slowly pulling it down over her large thighs, kissing the inside of them as he pushed the material down. Her brief panties came next. When removing them, he tickled her spur tongue with his little finger. He could feel it become hard under his professional performance.

70

Janet stretched out on the bed, feeling every nerve in her body demanding more and more of his flexible lovemaking. As soon as he removed the brief panties from off her legs, he glanced down and caught his breath. Here indeed was a rare flower. Her body was perfection. He surrendered to his basic desires and allowed his passionate temperament to take control.

Without restraint, he began to kiss her slowly on the stomach. He worked his way down and, before she knew what was happening, his tongue slipped in and out of her near virginal cunt. The feeling set her on fire. She had never had a man go down on her, and the feeling burst on her like rockets exploding in the sky. She couldn't control the emotions that beset her.

All at once she felt as if her body was on fire. She wanted to tell him to stop, but it felt so good she couldn't bring the words out. The next thing she knew she was stretching her body upward, trying to reach the elusive tongue that seemed to set her on fire.

Never before had she even imagined such a feeling. Her body belonged to someone else. It couldn't be hers. Her cries of passion rang out in his ears, and as he made love to her he coldly reflected on how she would pay for this moment of pleasure.

Ronald hadn't bothered to remove his clothes. But now, as passion became the ruling factor in their lovemaking, he found himself pulling at his jacket, almost tearing the zipper out of his pants in his hurry to undress. As she lay back, beckoning with her arms for him to hurry, he glanced down at the young body waiting for him and almost came in his pants.

He removed his shorts and his pants at the same time. Ronald didn't bother to lay his clothes out neatly. He just dropped them in a bundle on the floor. Quickly he mounted her like a stallion taking a mare. He plunged into her viciously, but no matter how hard he rode, she begged for more.

For the next ten minutes he rode her as if she was notoriously experienced, instead of a young girl who was being busted out for the second time. But she loved every minute of it. The harder he drove home, the better she liked it. He dropped his head and began to suck her breast.

"Harder, honey! Suck it harder. Bite it," she cried in her passion. "Bite it, goddamn you! Make me feel it!"

Her words filled him with desire and she moved under him like a wild animal. The harder he pushed, the harder she rose up. He couldn't give her enough dick. The moans that escaped from her came from somewhere deep inside of her. She was like another woman. There was no mentality left between them. They were two animals committing an act of copulation.

Her cries, becoming louder and louder, were those of a person possessed, not the sounds of a woman who had just started having men. She cried out for more and more, and the harder he tried, the more she demanded.

Sweat began to roll off Ronald's forehead in small beads. He continued to pump with a desperate concentration but it was out of his hands. Their mutual act was that of two animals who didn't care. It was just a matter of each one satisfying themselves. But Ronald was a pro. Realization came to him that this wasn't the way it should be. He should be in complete control, yet he wasn't.

He fought off the desire just to give himself up to sex completely. He used all the determination at his will and brought himself under control. Now he fucked with the precision of a machine. Each stroke was meant to bring her to the highest peak of enjoyment a woman could imagine. He loved her now with a cold, detached air, knowing all the while what he was doing, while she allowed herself complete abandonment.

He could feel her nails digging into his back. The pain was enough to bring him to his senses. If there was anything he disliked about the sex act, it was a woman scratching up his body. He twisted and turned, trying to escape from her nails, but she continued to rake his body in her passion.

Finally he managed to pin both of her arms so that she couldn't do any more damage. But even then he could still feel blood running down his lacerated back. He cursed silently but continued to fuck her with a cold, calculated attitude.

This was for the grits. If he didn't take care of business right, it would be all for nothing. He had to make her feel something that

72

she had never experienced before. And the more wildly she moaned and groaned under him, the more he believed he had achieved his goal.

For the first time in Janet's life, she had been overcome by sex. She couldn't control the trembling in her limbs. The joy that Ronald brought to her was almost too much for her to bear. She had her first climax while in his arms, and before he finished, he made her have another one.

She felt drained, as if everything inside of her had been pulled out. When he reached his orgasm, she could feel every drop of his sperm as it shot up inside of her and made her come again until she was overcome with rapture.

They lay in the bed side by side, neither one speaking. It was as though, if one of them spoke, the tingling sensation between them would be broken. For Janet's part, she couldn't believe what she had just experienced. Her mind was seething with wonder.

Something had happened to her that she had never thought possible. Now she knew why women did things against their will. At that moment, nothing Ronald could ask her would be too far out. If he was able to make her feel those same sensations again, she would do anything for him.

After a few minutes, Ronald raised up and lit a cigarette. "Hi, baby," he said casually. "You all right, girl?" He grinned at her, knowing that he had done his job well.

Janet smiled sleepily. "You know I'm all right, daddy. Damn, I ain't never felt like that before," she stated openly.

"I know, baby. It was the same way for me too," he lied easily. He waited for a minute, then said softly, "I'm going to have to get up from here and make a run, Janet. I got something lined up that might just get me a few dollars."

"Can I go along with you, Ronald?" she inquired quickly. "You know," she continued, "I hate just sittin' around in this damn place. It's boring as hell."

"I can dig it, Janet, but dig this. I got to go and pick up a young broad," he said, then hesitated, letting his words penetrate before continuing. " 'Cause I got a trick who wants to spend one hundred dollars with a young girl, just for a few minutes of entertainment.

"Now," he said, holding his hand up to cut off her flow of words, "I might have to spend a day or two with her if she makes this money for me, but I know you can dig it. A hundred bucks don't grow on trees, so ain't no way I can pass it up 'cause I need the money too bad."

It didn't take Janet but a minute to make up her mind. The mention of him having to stay with the girl for the next day or two filled her with fear. The last thing she wanted was to be left sitting around the empty apartment all by herself.

"Ronnie, what does the girl have to do? I mean, for a hundred dollars, it seems as if she might have to go through a lot of stuff that I don't know about."

Ronnie grinned, then caught himself. "Honey," he began, "it's not what you think. It won't take but five minutes for the guy to reach a nut. I mean, it's like takin' candy from a baby. But I wasn't thinkin' 'bout you, Janet. I know what you think about shit like that, so I'm not about to ask you to make the money for me."

She blushed, then said quickly, "I know, Ron, but I might want to make it for you. I'd rather do it and spend the time with you than sit around here worrying about you and some other woman."

"Well," Ronald stated, as he got up from the bed, "I'm going to take me a quick shower, and while I'm doing it I'll give it a little thought. Like I said, I didn't want to get you involved in this kind of shit." He slipped off the bed and hurried into the shower. His composure was about to give way, and he knew he would burst out grinning in another second.

It had gone easier than he imagined. At first, he thought he was going to have trouble turning her out. But it all fell right in line. Now all he had to do was set up the right trick. Tony, who worked at the neighborhood whiskey store, would be just right for it. The elderly brother was an easy trick. From past experience, or rather what his girls told him about the man, he knew Tony would come quick, and the man was supposed to have a tiny dick on him.

That would be all to the good. Now all he would have to do

would be to slip Tony the hundred-dollar bill and bring him around to the apartment. It wouldn't take him long to turn the trick, and once he was finished, Janet would be spoiled. The money would have seemed so easy for her to make that she would never hesitate again when it came to turning a trick.

For a minute he thought about her father but rejected the thought, reminding himself that he could handle the old man if push came to shove. He'd hate to hurt her father, but if Daddy Cool got in his way, he would just have to get him back out of his game.

In his business he couldn't allow no brothers or mothers or fathers to interfere with what he was doing. Pimping was his game, and no good pimp would allow some bitch's daddy to blow the game.

When he came out of the shower he was glad to see that Janet had gotten up. She waited until he started dressing before asking, "I hope you have enough time to wait until I take a shower too." She stared at him so hard that it seemed as if she wanted to eat him alive.

Damn, baby, he said to himself, you really have got it bad, haven't you!

"Naw, Janet, don't worry, you got plenty of time. I'm going to make a quick run and I'll be back by the time you get out of the shower, honey."

Before she could reply, he pulled her to him and kissed her passionately. When he broke the embrace, she was out of breath.

Janet stepped back and caught her breath. Sweet Lord of Mercy, what's happening to me, she wondered as she watched him walk toward the door. The slightest touch was enough to set her blood to burning, her knees trembling, her flesh seemingly to crawling with unbearable sensations. Never before in her young life had she felt like this.

As she stumbled toward the bathroom, she reflected on what she had let herself in for. She knew she had told him she would make the date that he was giving to the other girl, but she prayed that it wouldn't be for a day or so. That way, maybe she could get her mind in shape for it or, better yet, talk Ronald out of it. Maybe if she found a job somewhere, he wouldn't want her to sell her body.

That was one thing she could do, she reasoned. Get a job and give Ronald all the money. If she worked two jobs—she shuddered at the thought but continued to think about attempting it—she could help pay off his debts even sooner. Once she had his car notes paid up, they wouldn't be pressed for any money, and then maybe they could plan for the future.

She hurried with her shower. Taking a large towel, she began to dry herself. The sound of someone at the front door caused her to dry herself faster than normal. She stepped out of the bathroom and was surprised to see Ronald in the company of an elderly, light-complexioned man.

Ronald grinned at her.

"Hey, honey, this is Tony. You know, the guy I was tellin' you 'bout. He wants to spend a flat hundred dollars with some young girl, and I was telling him that he didn't have to go any farther. I had the finest young bitch in the city in my stable." Ronald flashed his brightest grin and turned to the man with him. "What did I tell you, Tony? Ain't she a fine young mare?"

Tony was staring at Janet as if he wanted to eat her. He couldn't believe his luck. Ronald had charged him twenty dollars, true enough, but he had also given him the hundred dollars to give the young girl. All he could do was nod his head and hope that the girl didn't change her mind. From the look of shock on her face he didn't know what to expect. She seemed surprised, but Ronald had said that she would go through with it. Fumbling around in his pocket, Tony found the hundred-dollar bill Ronald had given him on the way over. He held it out toward her.

"Hey," Ronald said quickly, "I'm going downstairs to the car for a few minutes. By that time, both of you should be done got together, and when I come back everything should be okay." He stared coldly at Janet. He reached over and patted Tony on the back. "Don't worry, my man," he said with a grin, "just as long as you keep your word and spend the hundred with her, there won't be no problem. Oh yeah, Janet, be sure and don't take anything less than the hundred either, hear, baby?" He flashed her his brightest smile.

All Janet could do was stand and stare stupidly at the old man holding the money. She watched Ronald walk out the door as if she was watching a stage play. This can't be happening to me, she tried to tell herself, but it was all too real.

The trick almost shoved the money into her hand. She stared down at the bill, then realized that she didn't have anything on but a towel. But after a second she knew that it didn't make any difference what she had on. She stared down at the money in her hand. Well, now or never, she told herself, and slowly let the towel drop as tears built up behind her eyes.

It took less than three minutes. As soon as the old man entered her, he let out a yell and she knew he had come. But it didn't make any difference to her how long it took. She knew what she had done and no amount of baths would ever be able to wash away the guilt feelings that she would now carry around in her mind. But for some reason she didn't blame Ronald. She blamed herself. She should have known better. She could hear her father's words ringing in her ears and, at long last, she knew that he had spoken the truth.

FOR THE NEXT TWO DAYS all Daddy Cool could do was lie around the hotel. Most of the time was spent in his room staring at the ceiling. His mind was occupied with the mistakes he had made. But still he knew he would have to do something soon.

After the second call from Detroit, he began to sit around the lobby all day until he had the man he stalked down pat. He knew when the man left and just about when he would return. The one woman the man associated with was a tall blonde who wore heavy makeup.

Despite the pain it caused him to move, Daddy Cool began to take exercise daily until he believed he was able to move fast enough to get away. In the early morning hours he practiced constantly with his throwing knives, though there was never any doubt about his skill.

He still had a tendency to brood over his daughter, Janet, even though he realized that was the cause of his being hurt. If he had kept his mind clear, nothing would have happened to him.

On his third day of recuperation, the woman named Sally who had helped him to the hospital came by. He met her in the lobby and bought her a cup of coffee. With the utmost patience, he finally got rid of her, promising to take her out for dinner on the coming weekend. Now more than ever he knew he would have to make his hit and be quick about it. He was becoming too well known. The elderly people sitting around the lobby were becoming overly friendly.

For the first time in his life he became worried about a job. He would have liked to be able to pass up the contract, but he knew he couldn't get out of it. He became nervous, worrying over small things. As a last resort, he went out and rented a car under an assumed name. This way he was sure of getting away fast if something went wrong.

Finally Daddy Cool made up his mind that today would be the day. He had his mark down pat. He knew when the man would arrive once he went out. So he set everything in motion. Taking his bags down, he paid his hotel bill, covering his rent until the next morning. After placing his bags in the trunk of the car, he drove around for a few hours, then stopped and called the hotel, having them ring the mark's room, even though he figured the man was out.

When there was no answer, he was sure things were beginning to fall into the pattern. The trick should be out with the tall blonde, and if he followed his usual procedure, he would stay out with her until at least two o'clock in the morning.

Daddy Cool drove back to the hotel and parked in the rear. He went around to the front, then walked slowly down the hall and opened the locked rear door. Taking the catch off the lock, he checked the alley where he was parked. He wanted to make sure no one saw him leave. His next move was to leave the key to his room at the desk.

Since he had just about completely checked out of the hotel, it would seem as if he was gone. He checked his watch, noticing that he still had about half an hour. He drank a cup of coffee and spoke to two elderly women who sat around and watched the television until it went off at night.

"Well, ladies," he said, getting up from the soft chair he had used, "I'll say good-bye. My bus leaves for Las Vegas at three o'clock, so I'd better be gettin' on my way. Wish me luck. If I win big down there, I'll bring both of you a gift when I come back."

The two elderly white women smiled at him, then one of them stated, "Be sure to watch your wallet. Pickpockets are outrageous in Vegas. My friend told me that you couldn't leave any valuables in your motel room there because the maids go through your luggage while you're out."

"Don't worry, I don't have too much to worry about anyway," he stated as he started to leave.

One more glance at the large clock on the wall of the lobby told him that he didn't have too much time. If his trick continued to follow the pattern he had set, he would be showing up within the next fifteen minutes.

Daddy Cool tried to walk casually out of the hotel, shaking a couple of old gentlemen's hands as he went. He waved at the clerk, then went out the door. He hurried around to the rear of the building and let himself in. Taking the back stairway he walked slowly up, hoping that none of the other guests would venture that way.

Most of the time the people used the elevator or the front steps. Most of them were too frightened to take the rear stairway. Since a few of the rooms had been broken into before, the back entrance was always kept locked and there was a definite tendency to avoid using the rear stairway by most of the occupants of the hotel.

Reaching the third floor, Daddy Cool opened the door and glanced down the hallway. It was deserted. He closed the door and lit a cigarette. Time seemed to stand still for him. He took out his knife and felt the keen blade. His nerves were playing tricks on his concentration.

Twice he thought he heard the elevator opening, but each time he glanced out there was nobody around. He placed the knife he planned on using in his belt, then removed another one from the harness he wore strapped to his back. As with the other, he ran his finger down the edge of the blade, testing the sharpness of it.

Suddenly he heard the sound of the old elevator slowly coming upward. He began to feel the excitement building up inside of him. The back part of his leg began to tremble as he waited impatiently.

The sound of the elevator stopping at the floor alerted his senses. He shoved open the door slightly and glanced out. The first thing he saw was the tall blonde getting out of the elevator. Goddamn it, he cursed under his breath, this was something he hadn't counted on.

My motherfuckin' stinkin'-ass luck! he cursed inwardly.

Of all the times for him to bring the cunt back to his pad, this took the cake! Even as these thoughts flashed through his mind, Daddy Cool stepped out of his place of concealment. He was committed now. Whatever happened, it would have to go off.

The tall, lean Negro who followed behind the aging white woman glanced nervously up and down the dimly lit hallway. The small lights set in the ceiling of the gray painted hall were adequate, but one of the bulbs in the middle had burned out, causing a dimness in the narrow passage.

Because of that very factor, when the man caught sight of Daddy Cool approaching, he never noticed the knife the slim black man carried. At first, he was startled to see the light-complexioned Negro, but almost instantly he remembered having seen the man sitting around the lobby, so his initial fear was quickly dissolved.

To him, Daddy Cool was just another of the forgotten people

who were living out their last years at the hotel. A nobody, a person you saw but just as quickly forgot.

So it came as a complete shock to him when he heard his date cry out. Still he was unaware of his danger. "What? What the hell is wrong?" he managed to say before his date fell back against him in terror.

"Please, please," she cried, and her voice began to rise.

In another second she would scream, Daddy Cool realized, and that was something he didn't want to happen. No noise was the best play of the game, so instead of taking the mark out of the game first, Daddy Cool knew he would have to waste time on the woman.

Desperately, she tried to turn and flee, even though no threats or words had been spoken. She saw death bearing down on her in the form of a tall, light-skinned black man. Before she could turn around, Daddy Cool made one of his swift underhand throws. The knife seemed to twist in the air twice before it came to rest between the large breasts of the woman. She groaned, then slumped over.

Realization finally dawned on the middle-aged black man. Even though there hadn't been any sounds other than a thump when the woman fell, he knew somehow that she was dead. His eyes grew as large as picture windows when he saw a knife appear in the assassin's hand. He put his hands out in front of himself and backed up.

"Wait, wait a minute, mister. Please, God, please. I can pay. I mean I can really. . . . Lord of Mercy, help!"

He began to scream as he saw the man draw back his arm and begin the throw. His scream was cut off as the well-aimed knife struck him in the heart. He gripped the blade sticking out of him, but it was only in desperation. His struggles were in vain as he fell against the wall. His body continued to jerk for a brief period. In fact, he was dead on his feet.

Daddy Cool didn't bother to look back as he hurried toward his exit. He reached the stairway before he even bothered to look back. He was glad to see that nobody had bothered to come out of any of the apartments yet. Closing the door behind him, he hurried down the stairs, praying that no one would see him.

His luck held out until he reached the last flight leading to the ground floor, then someone opened the bottom door. He froze on the stairway, holding his breath. Whatever happened, he didn't plan on leaving any eyewitnesses. Too many people had already seen him around the hotel, so it would be foolhardy to leave anyone alive who could identify him.

Anxiously he waited, but he heard no footsteps. Whoever opened the door hadn't bothered to come up. Slowly he began to inch his way down the steps, taking one at a time, making no sound whatsoever. He was like a large black cat, stalking his prey. Seething with the desire to hurry, he fought for control. At any moment, anybody could sound the alarm.

But the compulsion to run was on him. Knowing that the two bodies upstairs were already discovered, he wanted to break from his cover and bolt. Yet caution and experience made him use firm control. When he finally achieved his destination, he was surprised to find that no one was there. He had half expected to find a drunk sitting on the bottom of the steps. Instead, there was no one.

Daddy Cool spotted an abandoned brown paper bag. He could see the empty beer cans and other pieces of garbage protruding from the bag. He understood instantly why nobody came up the steps. Someone had just been too lazy to take their garbage outside and had set the bag down in the staircase. Daddy Cool let out a sigh of relief, then moved on.

He opened the door on the first floor and peeped out. Seeing that it was clear, he made his way quickly to the back door and was glad to find it just like he had left it. He opened it and stepped out into the welcome blackness of the night. His silent steps went unobserved, except by a passing alley cat who was creeping down the garbage-littered alley in search of his nightly game.

The two messengers of death passed each other, each involved in his own pursuit of destruction. One was already finished with his merciless mission, while the other still stalked the frightened creatures who in all probability would one day pay with their lives for a moment of carelessness.

Before leaving the alley, Daddy Cool threw away his last remaining knife. It was a long push-button switchblade that he had carried for an emergency. Now that he believed he was out of danger, he didn't want anything that might draw suspicion to him. He started up the motor of the car, and having wiped the knife clean, he tossed it into a trash container.

He drove quickly out of the alley. At times like this he hated to emerge from an alley. There was always the chance that a police car might drive by, and seeing a black man coming out of an alley was always enough to make them stop to investigate. But his luck held. The streets were deserted. He drove slowly until he reached Western, then he took it straight out until he approached the airport.

When he reached Manchester, he made a right turn and took it over to Wilshire. From there he reached the airport in a matter of minutes. One quick glance at his watch revealed to him that he had a whole hour to kill. He wasted part of the time out in the parking lot, cleaning up any prints that he might have left on the car.

Even though he didn't really think the car would be traced, because nobody had seen it that he knew of, there was always the chance that a passing police officer might have seen it parked at the rear of the hotel and taken down the license number.

So he didn't take any chances. The car couldn't be traced to him, except by fingerprints, because he had rented it under a false driver's license. After he was sure the car was clean, he placed the key in the ashtray. When he had reached the airport he had called the rental company and informed them where they could find their car.

As Daddy Cool stepped out of the telephone booth, he heard over the intercom that his flight for Detroit would be boarding on ramp six. Daddy Cool put out his cigarette, then picked up his bag and started slowly toward his point of departure.

*E*ARL WALKED AROUND the open poolroom with a hangdog expression. Daddy Cool now had been back from his latest trip for over a week, yet he still hadn't found out the whereabouts of his daughter. Earl's problem was just the opposite. He believed he knew where she was and what she was doing. If Daddy Cool was to find out, Earl believed it would break the man's heart.

He had checked and rechecked the information he had received from various sources. The older men who came into the poolroom and shot their games in relative silence at the back of the poolroom seemed to be sure of what they had told him.

For that reason and no other, Earl didn't know what to do. This would be the first time in his life that he had ever held anything back from his friend. But he couldn't begin to figure out how to tell the man that his young daughter had become a prostitute.

For the past week Earl had been dreading the arrival of his boss. He was afraid the man would be able to see in his behavior that he was hiding something. Angrily, he stared out the window, wondering what was to be done. The front door opened and both of Daddy Cool's stepsons came in, followed by their loudmouthed friend, Tiny. Tiny was a heavyset dark-skinned man, who was known to have a quick temper and who liked violence. On three different occasions Earl had to put him out of the poolroom for starting fights. If it wasn't for his close friendship with the two brothers, Earl would have barred him permanently from the place.

The three men came in, speaking loudly so that the girls working in the restaurant part of the establishment could see and hear them. Earl gritted his teeth. His mood was already a foul one, and with them on the premises it promised to get worse.

"What's happenin', Earl?" Buddy said as he came toward the

front table. "You look as if you done swallowed somethin' that didn't agree with you."

The other two men laughed while Tiny glared at the huge man. He didn't have any foolish doubts about whether or not he could take the big man, though. Common sense told him to leave Earl alone. There was something dangerous about the huge man and Tiny knew it.

The three of them started up a nine-ball game. In the next hour all three flashed large bankrolls, making sure half the people in the poolroom saw that they were loaded.

Now Earl knew his day would be spoiled. For these fools to come up with large rolls of money, somebody had to have been ripped off. Earl wondered if Daddy Cool knew about it. If he didn't, he wouldn't be long in finding out, once he reached the poolroom.

The three young men laughed loudly. At every opportunity one or the other of them flashed his money. The other men sitting around watched them jealously. The sight of the large bankrolls only made everyone envious.

"All right," Earl warned them, "ya goin' have to cut down on all that swearing or take it down the street."

"Damn, baby," Tiny said loudly, "whose goddamn poolroom is this anyway? To listen to him talk, you'd think he owned the motherfucker!"

Before the speaker finished, Earl moved in on him. He didn't waste any time with idle threats. He just burst into action. He hit the heavyset younger man under the heart with a short uppercut. The punch traveled less than eight inches, but nevertheless, it was a powerful punch.

Tiny grunted, then reached for the edge of the pool table to balance himself. There was no thought of putting up a fight. The young bully was almost unconscious on his feet. Regardless of his condition, Earl didn't lighten up. He swung again, catching Tiny on the side of the jaw. It sounded like a board being cracked.

Before Tiny could fall, Earl caught him under the armpits. He straightened the man out and leaned him up against the end of the pool table. He glared angrily at the other two men.

"Now, I don't give a shit if your stepfather owns this joint or not. I'm paid to keep order in here, and that's what I'm goin' do. If either one of you don't like what happened, take it up with your father. Until then, or until he says it's okay, consider yourselves barred from your father's joint, dig it?"

The younger brother, Jimmy, wanted to say something smart, but the brute force of the man in front of him gave him a feeling of fear that he had never felt before. There was no way of knowing if Earl would cut loose on them or not, and Jimmy didn't want to take a chance. He glanced out of the corner of his eye at his friend Tiny.

It was hard to believe that Earl had taken Tiny out of the picture so easily. Even though Jimmy hadn't had any doubts about Earl's ability to whip Tiny, he hadn't thought it possible for Earl to do it in such an easy fashion.

The older brother, Buddy, just shook his head. He had too much sense to get involved in an argument with Earl. Common sense told him that they had gone too far already. Daddy Cool would back Earl up no matter what they said. Earl's word would be taken, and it was possible for them to be barred from the poolroom for a long time. Now they didn't have anywhere to hang out, all because of Tiny's and Jimmy's big mouths.

He had cautioned them about flashing the money, too. The dope man they had stuck up would be getting various wires from fifty different informers, and it wouldn't take long for him to find out who was spending large sums of money. Buddy thought back on the stickup. Everything had gone smoothly. They had caught the dope man's woman at home by herself, and there shouldn't have been any problem.

She had given them the money, but that hadn't been enough. No, Tiny had wanted to have sex with the woman. So now, not only would the pusher be mad over being ripped off, they had added insult to injury. Tiny had raped the woman while the two brothers waited in the front room.

"Now," Earl's voice shattered his thoughts, "you two get that motherfucker out of here, and when your father comes, I'll tell him about what happened. If by chance you see him before I do, you can tell him for me."

"They don't have to tell me nothing," a voice stated harshly from the rear of the pool hall. At the sound of Daddy Cool's voice, all three of the men jumped.

Earl was the first one to regain his composure. "Hey, my man," he began, "we had a small sort of run-in a few minutes ago, brother."

"Yeah, I know all about it," Daddy Cool stated as he walked through the small crowd of men watching the action from the safety of corners.

"Good," Jimmy yelled loudly. "This sonofabitch had the goddamn nerve to jump all over Tiny here just 'cause Tiny made a mistake and cussed."

As Daddy Cool came around the front pool table he stopped in front of his younger stepson. "You know what, Jimmy," he said softly, "you're just about the biggest lying cocksucker I've ever known. And when I say that, boy, I'm talkin' 'bout a hell of a lot of lying cocksuckers!"

The sound of laughter broke out as the bystanders began to really enjoy the show. Most of the time it was just everyday affairs that came to them. They came out of their houses and sat around the poolroom to kill time. It was better than watching television every day. At least it got them from under their wives and mothers, who were glad to see them go.

Most of them were out-of-work laborers or young men too lazy to seek employment. There were jobs around, but none of the daily loafers ever sought employment. A few of them, those able to shoot pool fairly well, hustled a few dollars from some of the working men who stopped by at evening time.

After a sharp glance from Daddy Cool, the laughter dried up, each man attempting not to be caught laughing. Daddy Cool's cold grayish eyes swept the crowd. There was a deadliness in them that gave each man who thought he was being picked out a shake from an unknown fear. If any of them had been asked, they would have denied it on their deathbeds.

Fear? Never!

The long walk from the parking lot to the rear of the poolroom had taken its toll on Daddy Cool. He could feel the pain from his healing ribs, and that didn't improve his temper any. The sharp pain in his side made him aware of the damage done to his body from the beating he took. His anger became almost unreasonable as he started to take it out on his two stepsons.

"Both of you motherfuckers don't appreciate nothin' nobody does for you. I asked you to try and find out where your sister was at, but instead you come up here flashin' a small bankroll that you took from some goddamn paperboy and not doing what I asked." He stopped long enough to catch his breath.

Buddy knew what he was going to say before he said it. With all his heart, he wished he could make his stepfather change his mind. What he had feared was about to happen. A good thing was being blown for no reason at all.

"So I'm going to tell both of you how I feel. Now, Earl has already told you not to come back into the poolroom unless you got my permission, and I don't think that will be coming no time soon. So," Daddy Cool stated coldly, "since I'm not about to give you my permission on the poolroom, I'm going to add one more little thing to it."

He stared directly into Buddy's eyes. What he saw there gave Daddy Cool reason to hesitate on what he was about to say. Over the years he had gained a liking for his older stepson, and he didn't want to judge him the same way he would judge the younger boy.

"At first," Daddy Cool began, "I was going to tell both of you to go home and pack your shit. But on second thought, I've found reason to be a little more reasonable." Daddy Cool glared angrily at the two boys, who listened to every word he said as if their lives depended on it—which was close to the truth.

"Now, instead of kickin' both of you out of the pad, I'm goin' do it this way." Daddy Cool watched his two stepsons as his words seemed to rock them off their feet.

"Now, I want Janet home, but I can't find her. So I'm going to leave it up to both of you. You have got one week to bring your sister back home." He raised his hand, stopping the comment that the younger brother was about to make.

"I just want you to bring her there so I can talk to her, that's all. Now, if you can't do this, I want both of you to pack your shit and get the fuck out from under my motherfuckin' roof. Do I make myself clear enough?"

He stared from one brother to the next, watching them closely. He knew how close he had come to putting them both out but had caught himself just in time.

For one, Buddy was thankful for the second chance. His face was flushed and there was no resemblance in his features to that of the man who had entered the poolroom earlier. He believed implicitly that what he had always feared was about to happen— being put out on their own, with no means of support except for the income that they made off their notorious stickups of the neighborhood dope men.

The younger brother, Jimmy, was a different case altogether. He thought differently. The thought of being kicked out of the luxurious ranch-type home didn't fill him with fear. He was all too ready to step out on his own. Youth and a kind of bravado was on his side.

He didn't believe anything could really happen to him. Even now, with Daddy Cool glaring angrily at him, he drew himself up and sneered, revealing yellow teeth as he placed a hand on his hip and spoke sarcastically.

"Big deal. Now we're supposed to spend all our time checkin' out all the whorehouses to see where Janet is workin' at, then. . . ."

That was as far as he got. Before he could finish, Daddy Cool had moved across the small space separating them and reached him. Grabbing him by the collar of his navy-blue shirt, Daddy Cool pulled him close and slapped him viciously across the face.

"Boy," he said, and his voice was at a deadly low, "I don't know what you're tryin' to say, but Jimmy, this time you had better get it together!"

Jimmy, staring into the wild eyes of his stepfather, believed for a second that he had gone too far. But since he knew truth was on his side, he decided to play it for all it was worth. He tried to disentangle the hands that held him so tightly.

"Listen, man, I ain't got no reason to lie," he began. Then when he felt Daddy Cool easing his grip, he continued. "If you don't believe me, ask old black-ass Bill standin' back there against the wall. He done turned at least two tricks with her, so I sure ain't lying!"

The elderly black man called Bill tried to make himself smaller in the small crowd. He bent down; the last thing he wanted was to be put on Front Street.

Daddy Cool released his stepson and turned around and searched the crowd like a blind man. There was a distant look in his eyes. He was gazing at the crowd of onlookers, but even though his eyes were wide, it was as though he were blind. The shock of his stepson's words was still ringing in his ears. The truth was something he didn't want to hear.

In his private hurt, he didn't see the angry glare Buddy gave his younger brother. What Janet did, Buddy reasoned, was her business. He didn't like the idea of her turning tricks, but again, it was her business.

Earl watched the man he loved fumble around like a blind man. The hurt was too apparent. He was like a man in shock. "Bill," Daddy Cool cried, "Bill, you bastard! Come up here! I want the truth out of you, nigger, and nothin' but it!" he yelled, still not really seeing the man he sought.

Bill, on the other hand, believed that Daddy Cool was staring right at him. He came from the rear of the crowd, cursing his luck. The last thing he wanted was to face an angry Daddy Cool. When he reached the front of the poolroom, he held back, keeping a pool table between him and Daddy Cool.

"Yeah, Larry," he said, using Daddy Cool's real name. "I'm here, man."

Fighting back the tears that threatened to pour out, Larry Jackson managed to get himself under control. He focused in on the man he wanted.

90

"Tell me, Bill, tell me the truth. Is this young motherfucker lying?"

Before Bill could answer, Daddy Cool screamed, "If he's lyin', I'm going to make sure his young ass pays for this shit. I mean it, Bill. I don't play this kind of shit!"

There was desperation in his voice. For a second, old man Bill started to lie, but his eyes caught those of the younger man and his knees began to shake. He knew if he lied he would have to pay for it. The younger violent black man who had made the claim would wait for him outside the poolroom, and Bill knew at his age he couldn't handle the younger man. An ass-whipping was something he didn't need.

He dropped his head. "Yeah, Larry," he stated, "it's true. I turned a trick with her for twenty-five dollars. I didn't know she was your daughter, I swear. I just picked up a young girl on Woodward and took her to the motel. It wasn't until afterward that a fellow told me she was your child." He began to blubber. Tears of fear rolled down his cheeks as he saw the cold, deadly stare that Daddy Cool fixed on him.

"I swear," Bill continued, "I just didn't know. She's a fine young thing, and I was just spendin' some money. You can't hold that against me, Larry, you just can't!"

The man's words beat at Daddy Cool like sledgehammers. He heard them but didn't want to hear them. The man's begging was enough to assure him that he spoke the truth. Now the only thing he could think of was why?

The question kept ringing in his mind. If she needed money, all she had to do was contact him. So why be a whore? She wasn't an addict, or was she? This was a new perspective. If the nigger she messed around with had made an addict out of her, then he could understand it. But first of all, he would have to find out if this was her problem. Whatever it was, he would help her and take care of the person responsible for her problems.

"As for you," Daddy Cool stated, staring down at Jimmy, his younger stepson, "I want you out of my house today. When I come home, have your shit and be gone. If I find you there, I'm going to forget you belong to your mother and kick all the grippers out of your ass! Do I make myself clear?"

He stared down into the younger man's eyes, waiting for a reply that would be smart enough to let him go the way he wanted to go. He wanted to explode in violence. For one of the few times in his life, Larry Jackson was damn near out of control of his emotions.

Knowing that his stepson had this information and had kept it to himself helped to foster his anger. He didn't even consider the older brother; his anger was all for Jimmy. The smart-ass one. The one who enjoyed breaking such news in front of all the loafers in the poolroom. At that moment, Daddy Cool was gripped by an emotion to kill. He knew he wanted to kill, and it didn't concern profit this time.

"You scummy little motherfucker!" he swore in Jimmy's face. "I could cut your motherfuckin' balls out and enjoy every minute of your pain! But I can't allow myself that enjoyment at this time. But Jimmy, I want you to know, boy, from here on out, just because I live with your mother, that don't mean nothing. If you so much as cross my path, I'm going to try my goddamnedest to kick all the black off your ass!"

To retain his pride, Jimmy tried to break the grip Daddy Cool had on him. But for all his twisting and turning, he couldn't make the older man release his collar. Even though Jimmy was dark, people could see that he blushed from the embarrassment. He cursed wildly, his temper getting the best of him. Never before in his life had he been treated in such a way in front of other people, and his pride couldn't stand it.

"Goddamn it," he swore, "turn me loose! I ain't the one who turned her out, so why the fuck are you tryin' to take it out on me?"

Jimmy's words rang a bell with quite a few of the men watching. They believed that he was getting a raw deal. It wasn't his fault that his stepsister started selling pussy, so why should Daddy Cool take it out on him?

But Daddy Cool was thinking altogether differently. He didn't blame Jimmy for his sister's predicament. What he blamed Jimmy for was keeping it quiet. The young boy should have come to him at once with the wire that his sister was out on the streets. Then, between them, they might have been able to do something about it.

But Daddy Cool knew the makeup of Jimmy too well. He knew the young boy enjoyed seeing his sister out there, and that was the reason why he had waited, then tossed it into his stepfather's face when he had got the chance. For being that petty, Daddy Cool had decided to make him pay.

No more would he shoulder the responsibility for the acts the young boy committed. From now on when he got into trouble, he would have to get out of it the best way he could. No more would Daddy Cool send a bondsman downtown to get him out. Those days were over with.

"I'm goin' turn you loose, boy," Daddy Cool stated, "but just remember what I said. Act like we live in two different worlds from now on, 'cause if you don't, I promise you a world of trouble that you can't begin to understand that I can cause you!"

He released the boy, then turned to his older brother. "Buddy, you see to it that he gets the fuck out of my house. What you do is up to you; I'm not puttin' you out, so it's your choice." Daddy Cool turned on his heels and walked swiftly to the rear of the club.

Earl watched the two brothers pick up their friend and hold him up. Then they started toward the front door. When he was sure that they would go out without causing any more trouble, he turned on his heel and followed his boss to the office.

10

IT WAS DARK OUTSIDE, even though it was still early. Janet glanced up at the sky. It looked like rain. She prayed silently that it wouldn't, because if it did, it would make her business bad. For the hundredth time, she remembered that today had been her birthday. How good it would have made her feel had Ronald given her a small gift.

It wouldn't have had to be anything expensive, just the idea that he remembered. She had just told him about it the night before, but he had probably forgotten. His mind was busy thinking about his trap money, and nothing else.

As she stopped on the corner to let the traffic clear, she bent down and glanced in the passing cars. One white man stared back at her, and she beckoned her head for him to turn the corner. She stepped back on the curb and watched the car turn and then stop. She moved back from the crosswalk, staring up and down the street to make sure no police saw her.

It was funny, she reasoned as she approached the car, that one month ago if someone had told her she would be out on the streets turning tricks, she would have laughed at them. It would have been unbelievable. Yet, here she was out on the street selling her wares just like the rest of the black women moving slowly up and down Woodward Avenue.

"Hi," she said to the aging white man behind the wheel.

The man, nearing fifty, with grayish hair and a large potbelly, stared back at the attractive young black girl. He considered himself lucky tonight: the girl was young and exceptionally good looking.

"Hi, yourself," he said happily.

"Would you like to have a little fun?" she inquired, her voice dropping into a husky whisper.

"I don't know," he stalled, staring at her hungrily. "It all depends on how much the fun might cost."

"I don't know," she countered. "About how much could you spend?"

For the next ten minutes they seesawed back and forth. Janet started at fifty dollars, but had to come down. "Well," she stated, with her hand on the door, "if you can't spend any more than that, I had better be going."

"Wait a second," the man stated, panic in his voice. "I just might be able to raise twenty dollars, but no more than that. Shit," he continued, "a girl back on the other corner was going to go with me for just fifteen dollars."

"Well then," Janet stated, her anger rising, "maybe you had better go back to that other corner and find that girl. Like I told you," she finished, opening the door slightly, "if you can't spend at least thirty dollars with me, you better find somebody else."

The price was high, and the man realized it. But on the other hand, the girl was damned attractive. "I'll tell you what, sweetie," he replied, "I'll give you twenty-five dollars, but not a penny more."

For just a second she started to turn it down, but in the back of her mind she knew Ronald would have a fit if he knew she had turned down twenty-five dollars.

"Okay, whitey," she said slowly. "I don't generally go for that amount, but for you I'm going to make an exception."

The white man began to smile. He watched the black skirt she wore rise up around her pretty golden brown thighs as she closed the door. He couldn't take his eyes off her lovely legs.

"Hey, man," she cried out, "if you don't watch what you're doing, we're going to have an accident!" she said as he pulled away from the curb and almost ran into another car.

With patience, Janet directed him to an alley behind Cortland near Second Street. She had him drive up behind a condemned house and park. Now it was completely dark. She could see the glow of the cigarette that he smoked.

"Okay, honey," she said in her soft voice. "We had better get business taken care of."

"Oh, oh, yes," he said, then fumbled around in his pocket and tried to peer into it to find the correct amount of money. He pulled out a twenty, then couldn't find a five. The first bill he came out with was another twenty.

Janet slid over and put her hand on his leg. She ran it up between his legs and grabbed his tiny penis. With her hand on his dick, she began to beg, all the time playing with him. "Aw, baby, I know you can afford to give me that little bit of change. If you want momma to treat you right, you'll set me out properly."

The man's breathing came heavy. "Now," he began, "we already reached a price. I'm not going back on my word, so why should you go back on yours?"

Without answering, she opened his fly. But for some reason, she couldn't locate the small penis she sought. His breathing became ragged.

"Now," he cautioned, "if you want to enjoy yourself you'll have a little patience."

"Aw, honey," she cried, "you're not about to put this big thing in little ole me, are you," she whined in his ear. The words she said were the magic ones because he seemed to swell up with pride.

"Oh," he began, "do you really think it's large?" The note of surprise was in his voice, and she heard it and knew she had him.

"Large? Jesus Christ, honey, what have you been doing with this thing? You must have been a stallion for a horse farm!" By now she had finally found the tiny penis and began to work it out of his pants.

His chest swelled with pride. "Here," he said, and pushed the two twenty-dollar bills into her hand. "I'm going to give you a bonus, just because I think you will satisfy me," he stated.

She smiled to herself, then placed the money inside her bra.

"Okay, honey," she said coyly, "how do you want us to do it? The old-fashioned way or French?" If she could have stopped and heard herself, Janet would have known she had come a long way from the blushing virgin she had been just a month ago.

"Naw," the man stated quickly, "I like it the old way. Maybe next time we can experiment. But this time, I want to fill your crack up." He grinned in the dark to himself as he wondered what his wife would say if she could hear him talking now.

And how the hell would she feel if she heard this experienced whore talking about how large he was. It gave him a rare feeling of being somebody, even though every day he worked in the dull bank with dull people coming to him for loans.

Janet stretched out on the front seat. She pulled her miniskirt up, revealing her dark, silky patch. He mounted her slowly, his dick already hard, and she could feel something sticky coming out of the head. She prayed to God that he didn't have a disease of any kind.

Without any trouble she guided the small dick inside of her. The trick made two stabs, then moaned loudly and began to shake all over. She could feel him discharging inside of her. She tried to close her legs as he fought to pry them open wider.

"Open them up," he groaned in her ear. "Please, wider, wider," he whispered, filled with emotion.

She smiled to herself in the dark. It hadn't taken three minutes to make him come. She wished all her dates would be so easy. His penis was so small it was hard for her to tell if he was still in her.

"Okay, honey," she said in her false voice, "momma done took care of you."

"Like hell you have," he stated, getting nasty as he realized that his money was gone and he had come almost as soon as he had put his dick inside of her. He felt like he had been cheated. "We should go one more time," he began to beg as she moved from under him and sat up quickly.

"Yeah, man," she answered softly, "we can go again, but it's going to cost you some more money."

"More money hell," he swore, his anger rising. "I just gave you fifteen dollars more than I was supposed to. Now it's time for you to be a little nice to me," he stated, sure of himself, knowing that he would be able to handle the young girl if she gave him any trouble. He had made up his mind: either she was going to fuck again for no money or he would take his money back.

At the thought of getting his money back, he began to smile.

Even if she fucked again, he decided to take his money back. Why the hell not, he asked himself after glancing up and down the dark alley. There was nobody to come to her rescue and nobody to identify him. He had his mind made up on just how he would go about doing it. Then he turned around toward her.

It was just at that moment that Janet made her move. She hadn't missed his eyes as they swept up and down the dark alley. She was already afraid of turning tricks in cars, so she was always on her guard. She believed she had read his mind. When he turned back toward her, her hand hit the release button and the door sprang open.

She was out in a flash. His cry of rage followed her, but it was too late. With the speed of youth, she flew down the alley, then heard the car motor start up. But it was too late. She made a left turn and ran through a yard that she knew from past experience was always deserted.

As she came out on the street, she could hear the trick yelling. She remembered the flat pocket wallet he carried and regretted that she hadn't been able to lift it from the man. After once reaching the safety of the well-lighted side street, Janet felt at ease. She didn't believe the john would have enough nerve to accost her on the street, so she just as quickly put him out of her mind.

Swaying her hips in a flirting manner she swished down the street, well aware of the impression the passing men got of her. Ever since she was a child people had been telling her how cute she was. Being admired was nothing new.

As she walked along, she removed the ample bankroll that she had earned that evening and started to count the money. With what the last trick had given her, it brought her night's earnings to over a hundred dollars. The money didn't excite her. She was used to it. Her father had been extravagant with expensive gifts for her, so she was accustomed to large bankrolls. At home she had always kept pocket change that at times exceeded two or three hundred dollars.

Since today was her birthday, she felt like spending something on herself. She was still too young to have any apprehensions of overspending her trap money. Ronald didn't put her on any quota, so whatever she came home with she believed he would be happy with.

For the few weeks that she had been working, she realized that she had earned enough for him to pay ten car notes, if that was the problem. But her mentality was too high for her to have any delusions on that matter. Ronald was a pimp and that was all there was to it. He had turned her out, even though she still didn't quite know how he had done it so easily. Yet here she was, out on the streets selling ass. No matter how much contempt she had for herself, she did want Ronald and knew she would do anything he asked, just as long as she was able to remain his woman.

A car pulled up beside her. Simultaneously she flashed her new whore smile and started toward it, her hips swaying enticingly. Without a real close scrutiny of the driver, she opened the passenger door and got in, smiling brightly.

The smile on her face froze as she saw who the driver was. For a minute she was tempted to open the door and jump out and run. Wild thoughts ran through her mind, but for some reason she could do nothing. Shame was the main reason that she sat rooted to the car seat. She knew he had seen her trying to flag down other cars. There was nothing she could say. She dropped her head and stared down at her shoes.

"Hey, kitten," he said gently, "I didn't come down here to find you just to see you lookin' blue. I remembered that today was your birthday and hoped maybe we could have dinner or something together."

"Oh, Daddy," she cried; then the flood gates opened and all the pent-up emotions she had been holding back came spilling out. Daddy Cool leaned over and took his daughter in his arms. She cried as though her heart was broken.

As he held her tenderly, he had to fight down a lump that came into his throat. He stroked the back of her head and spoke gently to her. "Now, girl, it ain't nothin' that bad, is there? I know I raised a girl who could just about handle everything that came up."

Janet fought back the rest of the tears. She raised her hand and wiped the tears from her cheeks. "Damn," she swore, "I'm just ruining my makeup."

His laughter was soft yet relaxing to her. He hadn't accused her of anything. Soon the shame she had felt began to leave. She even managed to raise her head and look him in the eye. Daughter and father stared at each other. There was so much resemblance between them that a stranger couldn't help but know they were kin.

"Now, how do you feel?" he inquired. "After all them tears, I know you must feel better."

Janet tried another smile. This time it was the real thing, not the fake bright smile she put on for the tricks. Her heart was in this one; it was natural. Her whole face seemed to brighten up. Her beautiful teeth gleamed in the darkness of the car.

As the two stared into each other's eyes, a bright light hit them. Daddy Cool raised his arm trying to block out the light that was blinding him. "Goddamn it," he growled, "get that fuckin' light out of my face!"

"I'll get it out of your face, all right," a tall, uniformed white police officer stated as he stared into the car. "All right, both of you out of there!"

Cursing angrily, Daddy Cool shoved his door open quickly, catching the policeman's knee. The officer yelled and cursed loudly, bringing his partner on the run.

"What the hell is going on here?" the black officer asked as he came up. He stared from his limping partner back to the angry, red-faced Daddy Cool, who was glaring at the policeman he had hit with the door.

"Book this bastard for disorderly conduct with a prostitute," the white policeman said harshly. "We're going to run both their asses in and give this young whore a ticket for plying her wares on a business street!"

"I just wish the fuck you would run us downtown and charge us with some shit like that," Daddy Cool stated, his temper almost getting out of control.

"Daddy," Janet said softly, "now control yourself. The policemen just made a mistake, that's all."

The black officer saw what his partner had missed. How alike the two people looked. He was sure that this was a father and daughter, even before she called him "Daddy."

The white officer finally shook the kinks out of his leg. "Okay, you," he said to Daddy Cool, "get up against that fuckin' car and spread your legs."

"Wait a minute, Mack," his partner said. "I think there has been a mistake here."

"Mistake my ass," the officer roared. Both policemen were officers who walked the beat; each was still young, neither man over twenty-five. Mack had seen Janet working earlier but had not been able to catch her before she got in a car and rode off. Now he knew he had her and believed he had caught her with a trick.

"I don't know where the hell you were at, Bill, when we walked up. Didn't you see this bastard pawing the hell out of her in the front seat? At least the bastard could have had the decency to pull up in a fuckin' alley and do his dirt, but hell no, not this jig. He was gettin' ready to ball the little fluff right in the front seat on Main Street!"

"Goddamn it," Daddy Cool roared, as Janet clutched desperately at his arm, "you filthy-mouthed white motherfucker you, I'll have your ass for this!"

The sudden outburst surprised the angry white officer. The black policeman stepped in between them because he knew the angry black man in front of him was about to attack his partner.

"Now, you just slumber down there, brother," he said good-naturedly.

Mack was surprised by the actions of his partner. "What the hell goes on here?" he yelled. "I want this bastard in irons so we can put a call in and have a car pick them up."

"Just hold on, Mack," Officer Bill stated. "I keep tryin' to tell you we have a mistake on our hands here. This guy was not tryin' to make out with this young lady. This is his daughter."

"Daughter hell!" Mack exploded. "I'm not buyin' no crap like that. I know what I saw and I'm willin' to back it up in court."

"Well, I'm not," Bill stated. "I'll never be laughed out of the station every time I arrive for work. Now stop roaring like a damn bull and use your eyes, man. A fuckin' blind man could tell you this is a father and daughter here, so how the hell are we going to run them in on a charge of prostitution?"

For a brief second Mack hesitated, but he didn't like it at all. He believed he had seen them making out and didn't have any idea of changing his mind. "I know what I saw," he stated doggedly.

"I know what you saw too, you ignorant motherfucker," Daddy Cool stated harshly. The cuss words didn't help matters out any. The white officer got red in the face and stuck his narrow chest out like a bantam rooster.

"Now, you just slow down, brother," the colored policeman said. "I'll handle everything here."

"Naw, fuck that shit. I want you guys to run us in on that fuckin' charge that your partner dug up. I just hope the hell you do, so I can sue the shit out of the city," Daddy Cool stated, his eyes blazing with smothering anger.

Janet started to laugh, a soft giggle that began to build up until she was bent over with mirth. While she laughed, another pair of policemen came up. Only this time this pair was riding in a patrol car. They got out and walked over. In seconds the officer called Bill had explained what had happened, while his partner glared angrily around like an enraged bull.

The two new arrivals took one glance at the couple about to be arrested and laughed. "I wouldn't want to be the ones who wrote out the charge against them," one of the late arriving officers stated.

His partner stated coldly, "Just make them show some ID, that's all. That should clear the matter up fast enough."

"I don't have any on me," Janet stated quickly, remembering that Ronald had made her leave everything with her real name on it at home, so that if she got busted she could use a phony name.

"Well, there's your charge there," one of the policemen said. "She ain't got any ID on her, so you could take her down and run a make on her."

"I just wish the fuck you would," Daddy Cool stated harshly. "My daughter is only sixteen years old and if you motherfuckers take her down to a police station, I'll spend ten thousand dollars trying to hang your asses up for it!"

Now every one of the policemen stared at Daddy Cool sharply. They didn't like being threatened, but if she was under age like he said, it could become a sticky problem.

"I'll tell you what," Officer Bill said, "why don't you just get back into your car with your girl and leave? We'll forget this crap ever happened, okay?"

Mack glared at him hotly. He didn't like the idea at all. He was sure that the couple was putting shit on them. He remembered what he had seen and wouldn't change his mind.

"For myself," Mack stated loudly, "I'd still like to take them down and charge them, just like I said from the beginning. I know what I saw, and I don't give a damn how much they look alike. I believe they were carrying on unlawfully, parked right here on the fuckin' street."

"Man, man, man," Janet said, "I can see now they don't hire police for their brains, that's for sure." She stared right at the policeman who wanted to arrest them.

"Well, I just hope the hell you do take us down and charge us with some bullshit," Daddy Cool said.

Officer Bill shook his head. He wasn't about to let his partner shove them into something that would make them the laughing stock of the police station. The other two officers stood in the street undecided. If they were going to book the couple, it was up to them to drive the arrested couple down to the station. Neither man wanted any part of it. They could see the relationship between the father and daughter.

"Mack," the driver of the cruiser said, "I think you had better listen to your partner on this one, man. This thing can get out of hand, and I for one don't like the idea of being made a fool of."

Despite the warning, Mack still hesitated. He knew he could force the issue, but if he did he would be going against the wishes of all three of the other officers. He hadn't been on the force long enough to want to arouse the anger of the men in the squad car.

As far as the black officer he worked with, he couldn't care less about what his partner felt.

In fact, if he had his wish, he wouldn't even work with the black man even though the Negro had never done anything against him. He just didn't like the idea of having a black man for his partner.

Anxiously, Mack stared at the two white officers, trying to find support for his actions in their faces. Each man only stared at him coldly. It was obvious that none of them wanted the trouble Mack was starting. He tossed his hands in the air. "Okay, okay, if you guys want to let this fluff get away, it's up to you. I won't force. . . ."

That's as far as he got. Daddy Cool roared loudly, his voice drowning out the policeman's. "That's it! I've had enough. I want all three of you other officers to be my witness. I've listened to this ignorant-ass bastard insult my daughter too many times! I've had enough. He can't pay common courtesy to a black woman; well, I'm going to find out why he can't," he stated as he took out a pencil and began to write the officer's badge number down.

The officers stared from one to the other bashfully. They knew that now the shit was in the fan. If the man reported it, they would have to go up on the carpet and make out a report. Mack's ass would be in a sling, whether or not he knew it. Insulting a child in front of a parent wouldn't go down lightly with the captain.

"You wanted to find out if she was my daughter, well, you damn sure will, 'cause I'm going down to the station right now and report this. This officer has called my daughter a whore and worse, in front of me, and not just one time but numerous times. Even after I've informed him that she's only sixteen." Daddy Cool was breathing hard and there was no doubt in the policemen's minds now whether or not this was the father. They knew he was.

Bill tried once more to smooth things out. "Come on now, Mr. Jackson, let's let sleeping dogs lie. It's all been one big mistake, but I believe we can all forget it. No one has been hurt, so let's just go our own way."

Finally Mack realized that he might have put his foot in his mouth, but his pride was too much to let him apologize.

"Come on, Daddy," Janet said, "this has been a wonderful

birthday present for me. Listening to you give these officers hell was enough. Let's forget about it and go have that dinner you were promising me, okay?" She hoped desperately that he would do what she asked because she knew Ronald wouldn't like the idea of her going down to the police station. Once she did that, every time she hit the streets, one or the other of the officers would be harassing her or picking her up and taking her down to the station. Even now she knew she was marked. She wouldn't be able to work the streets here any longer.

Actually, Daddy Cool didn't really want to go to the station, but he would go if he was pushed. The less he came in contact with the police, the better off he was. Policemen had a tendency to remember faces, so it was best he kept his out of sight.

"Come on, then, honey," he said sharply, "I don't like the idea of givin' in to them, but if you insist, we'll let the matter go this time. But I can't stand any more of this shit." Daddy Cool waited for Janet to get into the car. "I hope you boys realize," he added, staring coldly at the policemen, "how lucky you are, because I believe I could have somebody's ass for this shit!"

None of the policemen spoke. They just stared angrily at the couple in the car. Each man was busy with his own thoughts. None of them wanted any part of the captain's office.

Daddy Cool started up the motor of his car. "I wish you would change your mind, Janet. I'd like to follow this mess up. I don't like the idea of them talking that way to you."

She blushed. It gave her a warm feeling to know that he cared for her that much. She knew that he had seen her working, but he never let on that he had. From his behavior, she reflected, in all probability he might not have realized that she was really working. Maybe he had just thought she was trying to get a ride. But his very next words made her realize how foolish this thought had been.

"If you're going to do that kind of work, child, you should try and get in a house instead of out on the street. Anything can happen to you, but I don't want to lecture you, Janet. You're a woman now, so whatever you do is your business. If you like that kind of thing, it's nothing I can do about it but pray that one day you will see the light and realize that you don't have to do nothing like that."

He removed a white envelope from his pocket and tossed it in her lap. "That's your birthday present from me. It's cash. I don't know, maybe you need it. I'm hopin' it will stop you from doing what you've been doing." He hesitated, then continued. "There's two thousand dollars in there, Janet. It's enough to keep you off the streets for quite a while. If you should ever need any more, all you got to do is pick up the telephone and call me. I'll see to it that you get all the cash you need." He pulled over and parked behind a cab stand. "Maybe it will be better if you took a cab home, unless you want to go home with me."

She heard his words and was tempted, remembering how safe she felt in his arms. She knew he was waiting patiently and praying that she would accept his offer. He wasn't trying to force her to come home, just offering it to her. But she knew in her heart she couldn't accept. She didn't believe she could live without Ronald.

Janet slowly opened the car door. There were tears in the corner of her eyes. "I'll remember, Daddy. I swear I will. And if I ever need anything, you'll be the first person I'll call." She took a quick glance at him as she closed the car door. For a brief second she thought she saw tears in his eyes. But she refused to accept such an idea. Daddy Cool would never cry.

That much she was sure of.

11

*A*FTER HIS DAUGHTER got out of the car, Daddy Cool sat silently behind the steering wheel and watched her in his mirror as she got into a cab. For a brief second he was tempted to follow her, but just as quickly disregarded the idea.

Janet sat back in the seat of the cab, huddled up like a small rag doll. Tears rolled down her cheeks, but this time she wasn't concerned with her makeup. If her father had only taken her in his strong arms and made her go home. No, she reflected, it wouldn't have done any good. She only would have slipped away at the first chance she got.

The way he did it was the best way. He was allowing her to make her own mess out of her life, giving her free room to make all the mistakes she wanted to. He had also told her that there would always be a place waiting for her. So she knew, if she ever got tired of the life Ronald was making her live, she could go back home.

But she had other ideas now. With the large sum of money her father had given her, it was enough for Ronald to settle down and take care of her. They had enough to buy them a small store or something. She daydreamed as she rode home. Now all they had to do was get married. She planned on bringing it up as soon as Ronald came to get his trap money.

This time he would listen to her. She would make him listen. None of his other women would be able to give him as much money as she carried. It was enough, she believed, for them to make another start. One thing she was sure of, she was finished with the street. There would not be another night like tonight. She remembered the shame she felt when she realized her father knew what she had been doing.

And then he asked if she liked doing it. He didn't seem to think she was doing it for the money, and he never mentioned Ronald, so maybe he really thought that she was doing what she liked. She blushed again. How could she ever get herself into such a mess.

But then again, she reflected as the driver pulled up to her apartment building, maybe it was better if he thought that, because if he knew that she was only working the streets because of Ronald, there was no telling what her father would do. She knew all too well how good he was with knives, because he had taught her how to toss them too.

So she knew that Ronald wouldn't stand a chance against her father if Daddy Cool ever got mad and called Ronald out. For all of his loud talk, Ronald would be like a baby against her father. She shivered at the thought. The last thing she could do was let him know the truth. No matter what happened, Daddy Cool must not find out that she had a pimp.

But it was out of her hands. Daddy Cool already knew she had a pimp. He knew about it but didn't know what he should do to the man who turned his daughter out. He had been around the game all of his life. In fact, when he was younger, he had had a few whores himself, so he was faced with a very difficult problem. As he drove slowly home, there was a fixed determination on his face, which, if Janet had seen, she would have been in even greater fear for Ronald's life.

No matter how sensitive the problem was, Daddy Cool knew he couldn't keep on ignoring it. He had put on a good act tonight, hiding the fact that he had been hurt badly when he saw Janet walking up and down the streets trying to stop tricks. He had to see it for himself before he could really believe it.

Now he had seen what everybody else was talking about. It was up to him to figure out what was to be done. He knew behind a life of experience who was to blame. His daughter had just run into a smooth-talking pimp, that was all, and in her inexperience she believed she was in love with the man. He could sympathize with her because he knew what the root of the problem was. Yet he hadn't come up with the solution.

When a tooth hurts you, you have it removed, he reasoned as he pulled up in his driveway and parked. After what he had seen tonight, there could be no more evasions, that he was sure of. Something had to be done, but what? The same thought kept springing back into his mind. Remove the source of the problem, then let the rest of it work itself out.

Janet paid off the cab driver and made her way upstairs to her tiny apartment. It was clean, but other than that it was a come-down for a young girl who was used to everything a girl could want. As she stretched out on the couch, she thought about how she had been planning on going to college this year.

It must have really hurt her father when he thought about it. They had talked about what school she would go to so many times in the past. He had promised to buy her a small car so that she could drive back and forth without any trouble.

Now as she thought about it, she realized that she had thrown all that away, and for what? To work the streets, lying down with any dirty old man who came her way. As she remembered what one man had forced her to do, she blushed. Holding her head while he made her suck him off, then feeling the stuff filling her mouth until she was choking on it.

The thought of it made her jump up from the couch and run into the bathroom where she was sick. After that, she took a shower, trying to wipe off the memory of all the men she had had. She couldn't scrub hard enough to make her forget. No matter how quickly they came, she knew she was in the wrong life. It was something she knew she could never adapt to.

Ronald would have to make up his mind. No matter how badly she wanted him, she swore to herself that she would never go back to the streets. The thought of the large sum of money she had for him made her sure of her stand. After he got that, he wouldn't be in any hurry to send her back to work.

After showering, Janet daydreamed about how they would spend the money together. Maybe Ronald would take her on a trip. How nice that would be, just the two of them. New York, or maybe catch a plane and go to Mexico.

Taking her time, Janet dressed with care. She was ravishing in the short silk nightgown she wore. Each time she took a step it flared out around her, revealing her gorgeous profile. Being really unsophisticated, Janet didn't have a hard time in making herself believe her daydreams. She honestly thought that Ronald would do what she asked. Subconsciously a warning bell went off, but she ignored it. She didn't even want to face up to the thought that he might not go along with her plans.

Every time she had a doubt, she remembered the money, and that would bring a smile to her lips. She spread the money out on the bed and recounted it. With what she had, there was over two thousand dollars. She decided to keep the money she had made and just give Ronald the money her father had given her for a gift.

The money was still spread out on the bed when the doorbell rang. She sprang up and ran to the door. As soon as Ronald entered, she threw herself into his arms. He pushed her back and stared coldly down into her face.

"Hey, baby," he said coldly, "I went up on the stroll to find you, but the bitches workin' up there said you had pulled up with some trick. What's the idea of you comin' in before I came down and got you?"

"Honey," she said breathlessly, "I got hold of some big money, and I knew you didn't want me workin' in the streets with all that money on me."

"Yeah," he said coldly, "just how much is big money?" He was still using his chilling voice.

Trying to make a game out of it, she beckoned to him. "Come on, honey, I'll show you," Janet said and led the way back toward the bedroom. She smiled brightly as she watched him approach the bed and begin counting the money. After about ten minutes of watching him, she realized that he was really having trouble counting it. She walked over to the bed as he set the money down and began counting it all over again.

"There's two thousand dollars there," she said lightly, watching his face for some kind of emotion. If there was any, it was anger that he wasn't able to handle figures. Ronald had always had trouble counting, and for some reason, he hated people to know that fact.

"Big deal," he snarled coldly. "It was a good sting, baby," he added almost affectionately.

"Aren't you pleased?" Janet asked, waiting for him to sweep her off her feet. He seemed to have changed since she had begun working for him.

"Sure I'm pleased," he stated, getting over his anger that she had discovered he couldn't count large sums. "How the hell did you rip it off, Jan? I ain't taught you how to sting."

"No, honey, I didn't steal it. My daddy came down and found me workin', then he gave it to me for my birthday present."

"Oh," he answered, and his mind went over what she had said. Then he thought of something. "Well, if your daddy gave this to you, what happened to the cash you made before he came down?"

"Oh, oh, I got that, Ronald," she began, then hurried over to the dresser and opened it. She quickly removed the money she had placed there. When she turned around, he was standing right behind her scowling.

"What kind of shit is this, bitch," he cursed, then slapped her across the face. "You don't hold out no money on me. Just because your daddy gave you a few funky bucks, you don't hold out the rest of the money on me!"

She was too shocked at first to think. It wasn't the slap that hurt, either. It was the ingratitude that he showed.

"I wasn't tryin' to hold back any money," she managed to say.

"What you mean, bitch, you wasn't holdin' back no cash?" he snarled. "If I hadn't mentioned it, you wouldn't have brought it out. I know what you were planning on doing with it, too," he added.

"What? What was I going to do with it?" Janet inquired, fighting to get her senses together. Nothing was going like she had planned.

"You were going to hold it and put it with the money you made tomorrow at work so that you could make me think you're just one hell of a whore!"

"Put it with the money I was going to make tomorrow?" she cried. The thought hadn't even entered her mind. She had believed she wouldn't have to work again. "What about the money I have tonight? I know you don't expect me to go back into the streets tomorrow night." She stared at him dumbfounded.

"Bitch," he swore. "Ignorant-ass bitch at that! You damn well had better go back to work tomorrow. Do you think because you gave me two funky grand that I'm goin' let you lay around for a week or better? Bitch," he almost screamed, "you must be out of your cotton-pickin' mind!"

Seething with an unknown anger, she stared coldly at her pimp. "You don't appreciate nothing I do, do you?" she asked, finally seeing the light.

"I don't know what you mean by that, bitch," he said blindly, not being smooth enough to see the damage he had done. "Bitch, I need fresh money every day. It don't make no difference how much you make tonight. Tomorrow is always another day, you dig?"

"Yeah," she answered harshly, "I'm really beginning to dig, you can bet on that!" she said as she put her hands on her hips and stared coldly at the man she had believed she loved.

Finally common sense warned him that he was trying to play the hard mack too hard. He saw at once that he was about to blow a good young whore and reversed his behavior. "Aw, baby," he said, taking her into his arms, "I was just jivin' with you. You know, the way them hard-ass pimps do in the movies and shit. You know I'm goin' let you rest up and we party. Now, come on and give daddy a big hug," he said and began to kiss her passionately around the neck and shoulders.

"It's a good thing you came to your senses," she managed to murmur between kisses, "because I was goin' take back my daddy's money and let you go your own damn way." She was being honest with him.

For a minute he went rigid in her arms, then caught himself. This bitch is crazy, he told himself as he kissed her again, passing up the desire to check her for being out of line. Take back the money, he reflected, almost laughing as he thought about her stupidity. The only thing she would have gotten for her troubles would have been an ass-kicking. But he decided not to push it. It was easier to make love to her, which was something that he really enjoyed since she looked so good.

But Janet was thinking coldly about her father's gift. It never entered her mind that she would have any trouble getting the money back if she wanted it. With the knives she carried lying in her dresser drawer, she had no doubt about her ability to take back the money, even if she had to make a pincushion out of him.

Ronald picked her up and carried her over to the bed. He had already picked up the money and stuffed it down in his pockets. He laid her out on the bed and then lay down beside her. He undressed her slowly, then took her roughly, making her cry out as he punished her for her ignorance.

Even as he made love, he made plans. It would be better, he reasoned, if he allowed her to lie around for a couple of days. All he had to do was keep his dick out of her after this. If she wanted any fucking, she would take her ass back to work with a passion.

That was one thing he was sure of.

FOR THE TWO BROTHERS and their friend Tiny, problems had been mounting ever since they had all moved out and rented a house on the east side. The rent was due and among them they had only twenty-five cents. It had taken the last money they had to get Tiny's old car out of the shop. But now they had it running and they were sure they would soon have some money.

"You sure?" Jimmy asked again, as they poured cups of cold wine and rode down the street.

"You better damn well bet I'm sure," Tiny stated. "We been watchin' that numbers house for three weeks now, and I'm sure we can crack it. All we got to do is go in as painters. I heard the woman talkin' in the store and she told the girl behind the counter that she expected the painters to come tomorrow and begin their work."

Buddy had remained silent all through the discourse. Now he ventured his remarks. "I don't know, man, it don't seem likely that they will open the door for us. She must know what one of the painters looks like."

"Sure, I don't doubt that," Tiny answered, "but the way I got it figured, all we got to do is wait until she makes one of her trips to pick up more money or tapes. Shit, once we see that little old green car gone, we know she ain't there, 'cause she's the only one who drives it."

"It makes sense to me," Jimmy replied quickly. He wanted some money and didn't care what kind of chance they took.

"Anything makes sense to you, Jimmy," Buddy answered sharply, then added, "but this ain't no toy, man. These people play for keeps. If we kick this joint over, we goin' have to play it mighty cool after that, 'cause they sure in the fuck ain't 'bout to forget us."

"Aw, man," Tiny said, "let's worry about skinning that cat when we get to it. For now, we got to knock the fuckin' joint off. After that, then we'll worry 'bout spendin' the cash."

In the next few hours they put their plan to work. All three of them dressed in white coveralls that were spattered with various colors of paint. Tiny stuck a small white cap on his head. Their first trip to the numbers house was in vain. They parked their car down the street and waited patiently until the woman they plotted on had left.

From his position in the front seat, Jimmy was the first one to see the woman when she came out. "There she is," he said excitedly.

"I don't know, man," Tiny replied as he gripped the steering wheel tightly. "It's hard to tell from way back here if that's her or not."

"That ain't no problem," Buddy spoke up from the rear of the automobile. "If she gets in the car then we'll know if it's her or not. All we got to be is patient."

"It's her all right," Jimmy replied quickly. "I can see her gettin' in the car." All three of the men strained to see her from their hidden position.

They watched silently as the driver of the car backed out of the driveway, then drove off in the other direction. Tiny started the motor up and drove slowly up to the house the woman had departed from.

"Man," Jimmy said nervously, "ain't you takin' a risk pulling right up in front of the house?" From the high pitch of his voice, Buddy could tell that his brother was scared.

"Hey, Jimmy, why don't you pull yourself together, man," Buddy ordered sharply. "It would look foolish if he parked anywhere else but right in front of the house. We're supposed to be the painters, right? So what the fuck, let's act like real painters."

Once again Buddy found himself put in the role of leader. Always when it came down to real thinking, both of the other men turned to Buddy for guidance.

"Buddy's right, Jimmy," Tiny said. "You got to be real cool, man. This ain't no chump action we gettin' ready to take off. This is the big time!"

"Right on," Buddy added. "Everybody check their piece, and remember, ain't no shootin' unless we ain't got no other choice." He waited to see if the others had any questions before continuing. "Now, let's be cool. The technique we're going to work out should be perfect. All we got to do is take care of the business. And remember," he warned, "as soon as I step through the front door, I want both of you to be coming in on my heels."

Jimmy and Tiny shook their heads in agreement as Buddy pushed on the car seat. "Okay, Jimmy, let me out."

Jimmy leaned forward so that his brother could push the car seat up. With a flip of his hand, Jimmy opened the door and waited until his brother got out. He could feel his legs shaking and knew he didn't have the nerve it took to go to the door by himself. If it was left up to him to start the ball game, it would never get started. He was just too frightened. He could follow orders, but someone else would have to lead.

Buddy walked slowly up the pathway that led to the front door. He was nervous, but other than that he was all right. His right hand went down to his waist. He felt the weight of the small .32 automatic he had concealed on his person. This was it, he told himself, this was the big one. Once they took it off, he would never again in life have to worry about asking his stepfather for help. The very thought of the security the money would bring helped to steady his nerves.

When Buddy reached the front door, it was another matter. A convulsive shaking began in his knees and he thought about turning around and fleeing. If he hadn't knocked on the door, he would have bolted and run. But before he could, someone opened the heavy inside front door and peered out at him. He snatched at the dirty paint cap he wore, removing it from his head. With determination he willed himself to use control. If he turned around and ran now, he would ruin everything.

"Miss," he began, noticing at once that it was a woman glancing out at him. "I'm the painter that the houselady requested to come over. We're supposed to start painting tomorrow, but I've got to see the rooms."

"Oh, yes," the woman replied, then added, "but you were not expected until tomorrow."

"I know," he replied, then added, "but like I say, I must see the rooms so that I'll know how much paint we're going to have to mix up tonight for the job tomorrow."

"Well," she began, "I'll have to check. Just a second, please." She didn't bother to close the door, but the screen door was still latched tightly so he still couldn't enter the home. The large red-brick house was just like the rest of the well-kept homes in the neighborhood, except for the doors. The front door was extra heavy. An old oak door that cost better than three hundred dollars. Two strong men could not possibly kick the door down unless they had some kind of tools at their disposal.

A tall, burly black man came back to the door with the medium-sized brown-skinned woman. He stared out of the door at Buddy. Seeing nothing but a young black man standing there, he relaxed somewhat and released the lock on the outer door.

As the door opened, Buddy wanted to glance back over his shoulder to see where his crime partners were hidden. He knew that they were supposed to be on the side of the house. His orders had been for them to come on the run as soon as he entered, so he didn't waste any time. He stepped into the house. Without holding back, he instantly went into action.

Snatching the gun, Buddy stepped back out of the reach of the burly black man. "All right," he yelled, "don't nobody move. This is a stickup!"

"What!" the man exclaimed, not wanting to believe his eyes. He stared at the young man holding the gun. For a brief second he was tempted to try and snatch the gun from out of the youth's hand. He didn't want to face the fact that he had been had.

It was too much. The very thought was intolerable. It was incredible. He didn't want to believe that this young punk in front of him would have the nerve to try to stick them up. What was worse, he couldn't bring himself to accept it. He moved threateningly toward Buddy.

As soon as Buddy saw the expression on the man's face, he raised the short .32 that he carried. Before he had the chance to shoot the man, the door burst open and Jimmy and Tiny came in. Both men were armed. They held their guns at the ready.

Seething with anger, the burly man gained control. "You punks will never get away with this shit. I guess you realize that, don't you?"

Buddy let out a laugh. It relieved him of some of the tension that had built up inside of him. "You let us be the ones to worry about that," Buddy stated, then pointed the gun. "Both of you get over there and lay down beside the couch."

Quickly Tiny and Jimmy had the man and woman bound hand and foot while Buddy explored the rest of the house. There were no other people there except a young, light-skinned girl in her early teens. She had long black hair down around her shoulders and anyone could see that when she got older she would be a beauty.

"Where the hell did you find her at?" Tiny inquired as his lustful eyes swept over the young girl's body. "Damn, but she's a fine motherfucker," he added, not concealing his desire.

The older woman moaned from the floor. "She ain't nothing but a child," the woman said quickly. "She just turned thirteen last week."

"Good," Tiny answered her slowly, allowing his eyes to roam over the mother slowly.

"Hey, man," Jimmy yelled, "we come for the cash, so let's get on with it."

"There ain't no problem there," Buddy stated. "It's all on the top of the dining-room table. You got the bag?"

Jimmy shook his head as he hurried past. A yell of delight came from him as soon as he saw the stacks of money beside the adding machines on the table. "Man, oh man, how the hell do you like that! I ain't never seen this much cash even at the bank." He began to shove stacks of money into the large brown shopping bag he removed from his belt where it had been folded.

"You," Tiny ordered the young girl, "get down on the floor so I can tie you up like the others."

The young girl began to cry as she obeyed the order. "Where the hell was she?" Tiny asked again, as he took out a dirty hankie and stuffed it into the older woman's mouth.

"She was back in the den," Buddy answered, watching Tiny closely. He had an idea of what was going through the man's mind and he didn't like it. "She had the radio going so loud that she hadn't even heard us come in."

Tiny only shook his head as he tied the girl up. First he tied her hands together, then he pulled the cord over to an old radiator and finished tying her to it. The only thing free now was her legs, and those he didn't bother with.

Before Buddy could move, Tiny ripped off the girl's white blouse. Her young tits stood out, not yet mature but still firm and hard. Before the startled eyes of his partner and the watching couple, Tiny bent his head and began to suck on one of the girl's breasts. He slobbered over her innocent flesh.

A loud sob escaped from the other woman as she watched her daughter being ravished.

"You no-good filthy motherfucker," the burly black man cursed, though in his mind he wished desperately that he could be the one enjoying the young girl. He had watched her dance in the den, and he knew she was a desirable young piece of trim, but it was a thought that he would never allow another person to know about.

Despite his dislike of what Tiny was doing, Buddy would only watch silently. The sight of Tiny loving the girl filled Buddy with a burning desire.

As the young girl twisted and turned, Tiny used one hand to rip her short skirt off. He didn't bother with pushing it up. He just gave it a vicious jerk and the cheap material tore. Next the silk panties came off. These he rolled down over her hips as she squirmed desperately.

"Oh, you dirty motherfucker," the bound man swore. "If I could only have a second with you, you bastard you!"

"Shit!" Tiny said over his shoulder, "what you really want is a second with this fine young bitch, you silly-ass nigger! You don't shit me, I know. You just ain't had the nerve to take what was in front of you, that's all."

As the mother of the girl squirmed around and sobbed loudly, Tiny took his larger finger and rammed it up inside the child. Her high scream was cut off as Tiny put his huge hand over her mouth. He didn't bother to remove his pants, he just tore the buttons off the paint outfit he wore and mounted her.

Buddy stared fascinated as the huge black dick disappeared between the young girl's legs. All at once a loud scream came from the girl, again cut off by Tiny's hand.

Jimmy came rushing out of the dining room carrying the brown bag stuffed full of money. He took one glance at the action and smiled. "Goddamn, ya puttin' ice cream on top of the cake!"

Buddy stared angrily at his brother, but in his heart he wished he had the nerve to fuck the young girl. But he knew he was too ashamed. If she had been dragged off to one of the empty bedrooms, then he might have gotten a piece, but he would never be able to find the nerve to fuck the young girl in front of everybody. He doubted if his dick would get hard.

"Hurry up, man," Jimmy said as he set the paper bag down and leaned over Tiny. "Man, oh man, you're sure puttin' dick to her young ass." Before he could finish the sentence, Tiny let out a loud moan and slumped over on the crying child.

Before Tiny could get up, Jimmy had his pants open and was kneeling down right beside him. "Shit, man, get off her. We ain't got all night," Jimmy said wildly.

Tiny rolled off the crying child and lay on the thick carpet. "Oh, wow," he moaned, "that's what I call tender pussy." The girl tried to scream.

"Momma, Momma, please make them stop, oh, please," she cried over and over again. The sound of her voice only added passion to Jimmy's burning desire. He forced himself into the tightly built child. Before he could really enter her, he felt himself coming.

"Motherfucker," he swore, as come came pouring out of him onto the girl's leg.

"Shit, man, you talkin' 'bout a sixty-second man. You wasn't on that cock a minute. Let me have another go at her," Tiny begged, waiting for Jimmy to get out of the way.

"If you do," Buddy stated loudly, "you'll be here by your fuckin' self!"

After making the statement, Buddy picked up the bag of money. He didn't even bother to look back because he didn't want to see the young girl. "I'm leaving," he stated again. "I came for the money, not to rape nobody, so ya can do whatever you want, I'm gone." Without waiting, he opened the front door, and after a quick glance outside, he continued on his way.

Struggling with his desire, Tiny pulled himself away. He cursed angrily, knowing that if he had had one more crack at the young girl, he would have really been able to bust her open. The second time, he reasoned, would have been longer and more enjoyable for the girl. He was conceited enough to think that he would have made her enjoy it, even though it was rape.

Jimmy followed his partners out, glancing back to make sure everything was in order. He also cursed. He would have enjoyed another go at the girl, but he also knew that Buddy was right. They didn't have the time for playing. They had come for the money and now that they had it, it was time to go.

Three sets of eyes followed their progress out the door. The young girl was crying yet thankful that her ordeal was over. Her mother was almost in a state of shock because of what she had witnessed. The burly bodyguard knew he had made a big mistake on his job. If it hadn't been for his stupidity, none of it would have happened.

But now that it had, there was one thing he was sure of. The three young punks would be seen again, and he had no doubts about that. He remembered the hidden camera inside the house. Everything that had happened was now on film. The burly black man shivered as he thought about the rage the girl's father would be in once he saw the rerun of the film with his young daughter raped.

Yes, there would be hell to pay, and some crying. But casket buying would be the order of the day in the near future.

AFTER LEAVING HIS CAR parked in the middle of the driveway, Daddy Cool staggered toward the front door and let himself in. Once inside his beautiful ranch home, he didn't bother to turn on a light. He sat in the dark, staring at the carpet on the floor. He had no idea how long he had been there; his mind was overwhelmed by the knowledge he had gained that evening. He could only sit and stare into space, trying to figure out which course should be taken. The thought of killing Ronald came and went until he got a headache from it.

That was the way his wife, Shirley, found him, sitting alone in the front room. "Honey," she called softly, then switched on a light, "why are you just sitting here?" She wondered why she bothered to ask such a banal question. That wasn't what she had on her mind.

When she didn't receive an answer from Daddy Cool, she continued. "Larry, your private telephone has been ringing like mad. I mean, I've never heard anything like it before. It's as if somebody had nothing more to do than sit at the telephone and just call this number.

"I know," she continued, talking fast in the offhanded manner of hers, "you've told me not to answer it if you're not here, but they kept calling until I thought I would go out of my mind."

She glanced at her husband and saw that she now had his attention. "So since you didn't want me to answer it, and I couldn't get any sleep with it ringing every five minutes, I went into your room and took it off the hook."

Her words rang a bell in his mind. Any other time he would have chewed her out for doing something so dumb, but now it was as if everything inside of him was dead. He just didn't care anymore. After spending a lifetime trying to get everything to give to his children, then to find out that it was all wasted. All the years of planning and saving, to find out that his only child wanted to be a whore. Or if not that, the money he had put his life on Front Street for would now go to a pimp who would run through it like wildfire.

"When I tell you not to touch my telephone," he stated rather harshly, "that goes both ways. It's just as bad for you to take the phone off the hook as it is for you to answer it. Neither action on your part is any help, so in the future, please do like I say. Keep your hands off it, understand?"

He didn't wait to see if she understood or not. He just got up and walked back to his room. He didn't want to be bothered with the senseless chatter of a woman who had a bird's brain in her head. He closed the bedroom door quietly behind himself and walked over to the nightstand and replaced the telephone.

He slipped off his shoes and stretched back on the bed. He felt if he slept forever he still would not get enough rest. For the first time in his life, Daddy Cool despised his very existence. What was his life for? He didn't enjoy it. And now, with his daughter going her own way, what was the use? He couldn't figure it out.

All the plans of seeing her through college, then one day giving her the kind of wedding a woman could be proud of were going down the drain. Where had he gone wrong? The question bugged him. Somewhere down the line he must have made a hell of a mistake to end up having everything fucked up. He might as well give the money to his two no-good stepsons.

It would be better if he gave the money to them than to see a slimy-ass pimp end up with it. His money, he had to laugh at that. People would kill for half the amount he had. He laughed again. People would kill: the thought stayed in his mind. He had killed to accumulate the money and now it didn't do him any good. Yes, maybe he had lived a good, or rather soft life most of the time, but was it worth it? He damn sure didn't enjoy it now. Death would be a blessing, he reflected, as he took out his cigarette pack and lit a smoke.

Before he could finish the cigarette, his telephone rang. "Yeah," he said, snatching the receiver off the hook. "What?" he snarled into the receiver. "Where the hell have I been? Whose fuckin' business is it where the fuck I've been?" he asked angrily into the telephone.

"Okay then, don't ask me no stupid-ass questions. I'm not in any kind of mood for it. No, I don't feel like coming over there. Yes, I know who the hell I'm talkin' to, but what the hell difference does it make? I could care less. Okay, you've had a hard time today, but so have I."

Finally the man on the other end of the line said something that snapped Daddy Cool out of his irritable behavior. He spoke with more respect. "Oh, okay, Big Jack," he said. "I'm sorry to hear that. I'll come over right away. Yes, I'm leaving now. Just hold on, I'll be there." Daddy Cool hung up the receiver, sat on the edge of the bed, and stared down at the telephone. "This is one crummy-ass world we live in," he said out loud.

He slipped his shoes back on. During the process of redressing, he remembered part of the conversation. Big Jack was a man like himself who had pulled himself up out of the gutter to have something in this world. Daddy Cool remembered going over to the man's house for Christmas, taking Janet along so that she could play with Big Jack's young daughter.

Even though Janet was a good five or six years older than Big Jack's daughter, they seemed to enjoy each other's company. Now, and Larry was sure of it, he had heard Big Jack crying. Yes, the big man had actually cried over the telephone. That was one of the reasons his nasty mood had changed and he had started talking like he had some kind of respect for the man on the other end of the line.

Daddy Cool was now impatient. He wanted to get over to his friend's house now and get the whole story. From what he had gathered, somebody had stuck up Big Jack's main numbers house. In itself, that wasn't too bad a blow because it was only money, and Big Jack could easily replace it. If that had been the only problem, Daddy Cool would have stayed at home. Numbers house stickups were numerous.

The drive was short, Big Jack's private home was just a few blocks away from where Daddy Cool stayed. Both men had bought in the neighborhood when a black face was a rare sight. Now, it was nothing to see blacks in the supermarket, but before, they had been very conspicuous.

Daddy Cool pulled up into a driveway very similar to his own. Before he could get up the walk, the front door opened. Jack stood there in his shirtsleeves waiting for his old friend. He nodded his head and led the way through the house to his private study. There was no one else in the room.

Before the heavyset, light-skinned man could speak, Daddy Cool spoke up. "I'm not really interested in taking this job, Jack. I'm retiring from the business."

Jack waved his words aside. "First, Larry, I want you to listen, then I'm going to show you something. After that, if your friendship means anything, I believe you will handle it for me. Now, I know the money ain't the problem. It's like you say, Larry. You're tired, so you want to step back. Cool, I can dig that, but first check this out."

Daddy Cool stared at his friend. He had never seen him so upset before. The man smoked cigarette after cigarette. At one time he had three of them burning at once in the ashtray.

"It was three niggers who knocked my joint off," Jack began. "Now, I'm willing to pay ten grand a head for each of the bastards."

Before Daddy Cool could interrupt, Jack waved him silent. "Please, Larry, just listen. It ain't about the money these motherfuckers took; it's what they did to my daughter. You know she still ain't nothing but a child. You know that, Larry, and these dirty motherfuckers had the nerve to rape her. Rape her," his voice rose, "and did it in front of her mother. The child is in shock now. Her and her mother are in the hospital. But that's not the important part. Ain't no bastard under the sun goin' do that to mine and get away with it. That's why I want you on the case." When he finished speaking, he picked up a picture off his desk. It was a picture of Daddy Cool holding the young girl in his arms.

Larry stared down at the picture. It hurt, it damn sure hurt. He had a little bit of feeling for the pretty child who called him "Uncle Larry." Yes, he cared for her, and it was like Jack said. It wasn't about the money. If the bastards had just taken the money and gone, he would have got up and laughed in Jack's face before turning the job down. But this was a far different matter. The child meant something to him, and whoever the animals were who committed the crime, they needed to pay for it.

"Okay, Jack, I'll take the job. I don't know what kind of leads you have on the people who took this off, but knowing you, I'd say you have a damn good idea who it was and where they hang out."

Jack dropped his head. "Yeah, I know quite a bit 'bout these bastards, Larry. That's why I don't know if you really will want to take this case or not."

Daddy Cool let out a grunt. "I just said I would, didn't I? Your kid is just like mine, just like Janet is close to me. I can't count the times your kid has stayed all night over to my house, Jack, nor the times my kid has stayed over here. So let's not hear no shit. I said I'd handle it and you knew once I knew the facts I would."

Jack stared at his old friend closely. "As you know, Larry, I got cameras all over my numbers joints. That way, if somebody gets sticky fingers, when I run the film back, I can spot the thief. Now, the camera picked up everything during the holdup." Jack stood up. "Hit this switch right here, Larry, after I go out. I can't sit through the fuckin' film again. When you finish with it, set it on fire. I don't want it under my roof!"

Daddy Cool stared up at his friend. Something was wrong here, but he couldn't get the message yet. He had a premonition that he wouldn't like it. But Daddy Cool followed his instructions and waited until the big man left the study before cutting on the film. The first thing he saw was his older stepson with a pistol in his hand. The cigarette in Daddy Cool's fingers dropped to the floor as he stared, shocked, at what was unfolding before his eyes.

The film showed Jimmy shoving money into a shopping bag, then all at once it jumped to the rape. If Daddy Cool had been shocked before, he was now dumbfounded. He didn't want to believe his eyes. He watched the abuse of the small child and tears of frustration ran down his cheeks. Now he knew why Jack didn't want to sit through another showing of the film. The big man had known all along that it was Daddy Cool's stepsons who had done this hideous thing to his family.

With a cold, chilling determination building up inside of him, Daddy Cool watched as his younger stepson viciously attacked the child. Now he did cry. Dropping his head on his arm, he cried like a child.

Big Jack didn't disturb him. Daddy Cool stayed in the study until daybreak before coming out. His eyes were dry by then. He found the big man asleep on the couch. He dropped an empty book of matches on top of the sleeping man. He knew that Big Jack would understand that the film had been destroyed. By destroying the film, Daddy Cool was letting him know that he would handle the job. If he wasn't going to do it, the film would have had to be saved so that the man who was hired for the job would know what the men he stalked looked like. Daddy Cool knew all too well what they looked like.

After starting up his car, Daddy Cool just drove around the city, moving slowly in the early morning rush-hour traffic. He knew it was going to be a grim job ahead of him, but it would have to be done. Men lived by certain codes and, when they were violated, a man had to make a stand. There were few things that Daddy Cool hadn't done in his lifetime. But he was proud of one thing: he had never raped anyone, woman or child.

As he drove he thought about Buddy. He couldn't hear the orders, but he could tell from the facial expressions that it was Buddy who had made them leave when they did. The film showed him picking up the bag of money and leaving, while the other two pigs were still on the floor. Yet, it wasn't possible for him to spare Buddy. Buddy was the one who did the leading, so he should have stopped them from committing the act of degradation.

If only he had, Daddy Cool thought over and over again, then they would have been home free. The money they probably could have kept. Since they were so close, Big Jack might have overlooked it. But not now. There was no possible way for him to overlook it. And if he had, Daddy Cool knew in his heart that he wouldn't be able to overlook it. The damage had been done, and now it was payback time.

Before long he found himself out on Bell Drive. It had been years since he had come this way. He parked his car and got out. Daddy Cool walked down to the water and stared out over it. How quiet it seemed out on the lake, he reflected as he watched the large ships slowly passing. How nice it would be to be on one of them, going somewhere, away from the madness that appeared suddenly everywhere around him.

After about an hour of quiet reflection, Daddy Cool made up his mind. There was no use putting something off that he could take care of now. The longer he postponed it, the more he would brood about it. When he returned to his car, he drove straight home.

He removed his clothes and redressed slowly. This time he took exceptional care about what he wore. Everything was jet black. The harness he strapped to his back carried six knives in it. He didn't believe he would need so many weapons, but he didn't want to take any chances.

When he finished with the hateful job that was before him, he would destroy everything that reminded him of his work. Before he left the house, he picked up the telephone and made arrangements for an airplane trip to the Bahamas. It was time for him to take a badly needed vacation.

Instead of telling his wife about his trip, he decided just to leave, so he packed a suitcase. He knew that after making the hits on her sons, he wouldn't like staring into her grief-stricken face. She wouldn't know why they had died, or care. Nor would she know who had done it.

"Shirley," he called when he reached the hallway. He waited patiently until she got up and came to the door. "I'm takin' a little trip, honey, so I'll call you when I get settled. If you should need any money, you'll find plenty of cash in the bottom drawer. Use the small key I gave you for my strongbox and get whatever you might need out of it."

"Okay, daddy," she answered, wondering why he seemed so strange. To her surprise, he leaned over and kissed her on her lips. It was the first kiss between them in over ten years. As she watched him walk slowly toward the door, she was surprised at what she saw. "My," she reflected, "he's gettin' old. I've never noticed it before."

For a reason she could not name, she followed him out of the house and walked as far as the porch with him. She didn't know what to say. Like always, when she found herself with him, she was at a loss for words, but she wanted to see him out. It was as though he was ill and she worried about his health. But she knew he was in perfect health.

She didn't want to even think about the idea that flashed through her mind. She remembered what her grandmother used to say about her husband when he had grown old. "He's got death on him, you can see it. Whenever you live with a man, after a long time, a woman can see things like that." She had never believed it before, and when the idea came into her head she quickly shook it off.

128

Daddy Cool waved back at her as he slowly drove out of the driveway. He couldn't really understand his own behavior. He blamed it on the job ahead. He knew he was about to kill her children and felt pity for the woman who had shared most of her adult life with him.

Because of his steady use of informers, Daddy Cool knew right where his stepsons were staying, even though they hadn't bothered to give him the address. It was located on the east side. He drove onto the freeway and noticed that the traffic had lightened up. It was after eight o'clock in the morning, and most of the factory workers were already at work. Now it was the white-collar workers who were rushing to make their morning time-cards right.

The house he stopped in front of was old and painted gray. The three men had the whole downstairs to themselves. As Daddy Cool made his way up the sidewalk, he prayed that they didn't have any company. It would be nasty if every one of them had a broad sleeping with them.

He pushed the bell outside the door. When Daddy Cool didn't get any answer, he raised his fist and knocked very hard. In a minute he heard a sleepy voice inquire, "Who the hell is it?"

"It's your pa," Daddy Cool answered, recognizing Buddy's voice. The young man answered the door, still wearing his silk underwear. He tried to conceal the small automatic pistol he carried. When he saw his stepfather staring at the gun, he shrugged. "You know how it is, Larry; in a neighborhood like this, you can't take too many chances."

"Yeah, I know," Daddy Cool replied, just as Jimmy came out of his room. So far, it was good. He hadn't seen any women. But that didn't mean anything. They could still be in the bedrooms sleeping.

Tiny opened the door of his room and glanced out. Daddy Cool noticed that the man held a pistol in his hand. When he saw who it was, he tossed the gun back into the bedroom and came out. All three of the men were wondering why Daddy Cool had bothered to wake them up at such an hour.

Buddy was the only one who thought he knew the reason. He

had known the numbers man they knocked off was a personal friend of Daddy Cool's, but for the life of him he couldn't understand how Daddy Cool might know they had taken the job off.

"What's the deal?" Tiny inquired, then staggered toward the toilet. "Shit, that fuckin' beer we drank done kept me pissin' all night." He spoke in the offhanded manner of a man who had just awakened from a mean drunk and wanted to impress everybody around him with the fact.

Daddy Cool let him take two steps toward the toilet, then reached behind his neck. The knife came out like a blur, striking Tiny right between the shoulder blades. Tiny grunted from the pain, then staggered toward the door. He fell up against the wall and slid down before rolling over on his side. On his face was an expression of dismay, as if he was asking how this could have happened.

The two brothers stared at the body dumbfounded. Neither man spoke. They still couldn't put it together. Daddy Cool removed a small snapshot he had taken from Big Jack's house. It showed Tiny tearing off the young girl's skirt. He pushed the picture under Buddy's nose while holding out another one to Jimmy. The picture he gave Jimmy was one of Jimmy straddling the girl. Jimmy's face changed color. He belched loudly, and for a second he was scared he would mess on himself.

As of yet, neither brother had any fear for their lives. True, they had seen their friend and partner killed right before their eyes, but they still thought the bond between them and their stepfather was too tight for them to have any fear.

As Daddy Cool removed his second knife, he stared coldly into Buddy's face. He saw the automatic sitting on the edge of the end table where Buddy had placed it. "Why, Buddy, why?"

Buddy could only shake his head. Jimmy, on the other hand, was beginning to realize their danger. He decided to inch his way into the bedroom and get his gun, then he could face Daddy Cool on a more equal level. Daddy Cool allowed him to reach the bedroom, then he made his move. His hand came up in a forward flip, the knife made two turns before embedding itself in Jimmy's chest.

Jimmy's eyes seemed as if they would pop out. He stared down toward the strange thing sticking out of him. He couldn't believe it. He reached out toward his stepfather, his hand beckoning, begging, pleading, but there was no kindness in the chilling black eyes that stared right back at him.

"I guess," Buddy began, "it's my turn next, huh?" he asked, not attempting to make any move toward the gun on the table.

Daddy Cool stared at the young black man in front of him. All he could see was his wife's face. After so many years of dedication, he owed her something, didn't he?

"How much money was in the ripoff?" Daddy Cool asked slowly, as he reached for another knife.

Buddy followed his movements with his eyes, he knew his stepfather was giving him a chance to try for the gun if he wanted to. "We took off twenty-five grand," Buddy answered, not even looking at his gun.

For a second the two men stared at each other, then the elderly one spoke. "You went along with a nasty thing, boy, something that should be with you until you reach your grave." Daddy Cool hesitated, then shoved the knife back down in its sheath.

"You don't deserve it, Buddy, but I'm goin' give it to you. Since you didn't touch the child and stopped them from abusing her further, I'm going to let that be in your favor. I don't know if the people you ripped off will accept it or not, but as far as I'm concerned, the contract is completed.

"What you do, boy, is get the money and get as far away from here as you can. Don't even stay for your brother's funeral. It might end up being yours also. So start running and maybe one day you and me both will be thankful for what's happenin'. I don't know. I know your mother deserves more than a double funeral. When your mother talks to you, I hope you will keep this between us. It won't help matters if she knows I'm the one who made Jimmy pay for his ugliness."

Buddy stared down at the floor. He didn't answer, just thanked the Lord that he was still alive. He knew that he had been closer to death than ever before in his life. When he heard the door close, he looked up. The house was empty. He hurried toward the bedroom. It wouldn't take him long to get out. He could call his mother from the airport. He decided not to take any chances. Maybe Daddy Cool wouldn't change his mind, but if he did, Buddy would be taking the man's words and putting as many miles between him and death as he possibly could.

IF THERE WAS ONE thing Earl hated, it was having to be out in the streets. Now, standing in the dimly lit hallway, he wished that the man he waited for would come on out. He had waited all night, after making up his mind on what had to be done. There was no other choice that he could see. If things continued the way they were going, his only friend would end up worrying himself to death.

The decision that Earl had come to hadn't been reached lightly. He knew that Daddy Cool might be mad about it, but once it was over with, there wouldn't be anything anyone could do about it.

Though Earl didn't know much about women, he knew that Janet was doing something she wouldn't ordinarily do. She was no whore, and there was no reason for her to be out on the streets hustling her body. From all he could find out on the subject, the person responsible for a young girl being out on the street was her pimp. If you eliminated the pimp, there was no cause for her to work.

He heard a door open and close on the floor under him and swore under his breath. The few people who had come past him in the dimly lit hallway had moved away swiftly after getting a look at the huge man. The sweater he wore had a hood on it covering his head so that people who passed by couldn't see how deformed he really was—but his mere presence was enough.

How Earl wished for the quietness of his small room. But if he had to sit out in the hallway until evening time, he would be there. For a second he worried about the pool hall. If he wasn't there by nine o'clock, how would the girls get in to open up the restaurant?

For the next half hour he worried over it, wondering if he should leave and open up the club, then return. It would mean exposing himself to the daylight traffic. People hurrying nowhere would stare at him as if he had just crawled out from under a log.

Earl glanced at his watch. It was almost nine o'clock. He remembered some of the men joking in the poolroom about how late pimps and whores slept. He couldn't believe they really stayed in the bed until two and three in the afternoon. At any rate, he didn't believe Ronald would. The man had arrived at the apartment building one jump ahead of Earl. Earl had had a problem finding the right building. If only he had been quicker he could have finished his job last night. Now it was daybreak and people would be up and around.

Even as the thought flashed through his mind, a door down the hall from where he stood opened and three small children came running out. Two of them carried small books in their arms, so he knew that they were on their way to school.

At times, children were even harder to stand than the grown-up counterparts who were deliberately cruel. While the children didn't really mean any harm, their hard stares and cold remarks hurt him to the quick. Now as the children came abreast of him, he noticed that there were two little girls and one boy. They glanced at him curiously, but he managed to turn his back so that they couldn't really see him clearly.

Down the hall in Janet's apartment, Ronald dressed slowly. He had made up his mind to allow her to take a few days off, but this shit she kept talking about was bugging the hell out of him. He had no intention of getting a job or buying a store, and he was tired of lying to her about it. He was tempted to tell her the truth, yet he was afraid he might lose her. He had heard guys talk about hundred-dollar girls, but she was the first one he had ever had. Ever since Janet hit the streets, she averaged a hundred dollars a night.

"Please, Ronald," she begged, "at least say you'll give it a try. Let me try and find a nice small store somewhere, and I'm sure if we need a little more money, Daddy will gladly loan it to us."

She waited silently, hoping that he would see it her way. Together they could move mountains, she believed, but Ronald just needed guidance.

"Listen, baby," he said, feeling the huge roll of money in his pocket. It made him feel free-spirited. "Why don't you take some of this cash and go shopping today, you know, just get out of the apartment and enjoy yourself?"

She smiled and shook her head. It sounded nice, but instead of buying something for herself she would surprise him and buy something nice for him. "Okay, Ronald, if you say so," she replied quietly, then waited while he pulled the bankroll out and peeled off a ten.

She stared at the ten-dollar bill as if it was a snake. Ronald, too caught up in his own importance, didn't even notice the disappointment on her face.

"Yeah, Jan," he said, "since I didn't get you a gift yesterday, you buy something nice with this."

For a second she was afraid to speak. She didn't want to reveal her disappointment. After all, she had given him twenty-one hundred dollars. It wouldn't have hurt him to be a little more generous. Staying with a man was one sure way of really finding out things about him, she reasoned, as she watched him put the money back in his pocket.

"Maybe you had better take this with you," she couldn't stop herself from saying, as she held the ten-dollar bill out to him. She was sure of one thing. She definitely wasn't about to go through all the trouble of going downtown just to spend ten dollars.

"Hey, honey, what's the deal? You don't appreciate the little bread I gave you? Oh yeah, okay, Janet, I remember, you're the little rich girl. You're used to spendin' them big, aren't you?" There was envy in his voice, something he couldn't hide. All his life he had to struggle for his. But here was a little bitch who had everything put out on a platter for her. She needed dogging, or so he reasoned.

That way, he would be able to control her better. If he was good to her, she would take softness for weakness, something he wasn't planning on allowing to ever happen.

"It's not that, Ronald. I'm just not used to tryin' to shop with such a small piece of money, that's all. I don't think I'd know where to begin," she stated, then flashed him a smile, trying to take the sting out of her words.

"Oh, you wouldn't, huh? Maybe you'd feel better if I gave you back a grand for you to go shoppin' with. Would that make you feel better?"

"No, no, Ronald, I don't want nothing like that, honey. I gave the money to you, for you to do whatever you want with it. So I wouldn't think of takin' it downtown and wasting it on clothes when I already have plenty of them."

Ronald stared at her with surprise. This silly bitch really thought I was serious about giving her back that much money. He shook his head. He didn't think he would ever be able to figure her out.

Seeing the look on his face, she stood up on her toes and put her arms around his neck. She tried to kiss him, but he didn't want any part of that. The lovemaking they had that morning was enough for him. And anyway, the good, hard, older pimps said the less you showed your affection, the more they loved you.

It was a bad habit letting a whore kiss her man on the mouth. And anyway, he could never get it out of his mind that the women who worked the streets for him had more than likely sucked a dozen dicks that night and swallowed a bucket of come. No, the very thought of it made him turn his cheek to her.

Janet wasn't anybody's fool. She noticed most small things, and she saw the way he acted when she wanted to kiss. She remembered how he had forced her to make love to him with her mouth, telling her that he was teaching her something she needed to know. Now she was putting it all together and she figured that was the reason he didn't want her to kiss him on the mouth.

As she thought about it, she decided that he had had his first and last oral love from her. She would be damned if she would go down on any man and then have him treat her as if she had done something dirty.

Noticing the look on her face, Ronald thought it was over the money. He pulled out another bill. But seeing that this one was a twenty, he wished that he had fished out a ten instead. "Here, girl, I want you to buy something nice today, so that when I come back you can really surprise me."

This time, Janet didn't even bother to glance at the bill he gave her. She just balled it up and tossed it on the dresser.

Now that he had freed himself from the bear hug she had on his neck, Ronald made ready to go. For some reason, he felt out of place when he was with her. She gave him a feeling of being inferior. "I'll give you a call around six o'clock tonight, Janet, so be sure to be back by then. You never can tell what might jump off." He smiled, then tried to crack a joke with her. "Maybe one of those hundred-dollar-ass tricks might inquire about your whereabouts, and you know we don't want to pass up any of them."

She caught herself before she said something nasty to him. Janet started toward the door. For the first time in her life, she was glad to see him leave. She needed time to think.

Ronald followed her to the door, wondering now what the problem was. She was just too motherfuckin' moody, he reflected as he stopped in the doorway. "Remember what I said now," he warned, his voice going cold. "I'm not joking about them hundred-dollar tricks."

Janet just held the door open. She didn't bother to answer. She watched him go, torn between her love for him and her common sense.

Ronald hesitated in the doorway, staring at her. She was a lovely picture in her short, black slip. The top of it hung down just enough to reveal her well-developed breasts, which, with no bra, stood out proudly. Any other man would have been overcome with pride, but Ronald's ego was so large that he never took into consideration what a jewel he had.

Seething from an unknown anger, he turned on his heel and

walked away from her, never bothering to glance back at the vision of loveliness he left behind.

15

AFTER FULFILLING TWO-thirds of his contract, the professional assassin made his way back to his car. Daddy Cool felt better now. After sparing Buddy's life, he believed he had done the right thing. He promised himself that he would make a call and explain it to Big Jack. Then it would be out of his hands. He wouldn't plead for Buddy's life though; he would leave that decision up to Jack. Maybe it would have been better if he had collected Big Jack's money, but since Big Jack owed him for the contract, he would just write it off as even.

It would be nice to have breakfast with Janet, he thought, and instantly began to consider how he could contact her. She hadn't given him any address, but it still wouldn't be hard for him to find out where she stayed. A few calls would solve that problem. At the first pay telephone, he stopped and got out. After three calls he had her address written down with the number of her apartment.

He would surprise her this morning. He glanced at his watch. It was still early, but since she had gone in early she should be getting up around now. It was just a little past nine, a good time for them to go and find a restaurant that served good pancakes, something both of them liked.

As he drove slowly back across the city, events were taking place that would involve him directly.

Earl, still waiting in the hallway, was about to give up. The old woman down the hall had glanced out of her apartment twice, each time seeing the huge man lurking around. The last time she saw him, her imagination got the best of her.

She believed the huge man was just waiting for the chance to break into her place. She went to the telephone and dialed the nearest police station. When she got the dispatcher on the line, she told him that there was a big man hiding in her hallway and acting strange.

Before Earl could make up his mind to leave, the door he had watched at night came open and Ronald walked swiftly down the hall. Earl pressed himself against the stairway, waiting in ambush for the younger man.

Ronald was almost upon Earl before he saw the huge man standing there. Instantly, fear leaped into his eyes. He stopped and stared at him in horror. Earl stepped away from the wall. Two more steps and he was in front of the frightened Ronald. His huge hand shot out and gathered some of Ronald's shirt in his grip.

At first, Ronald attempted to struggle, but his young strength was impotent against the huge man. Without hesitation, Earl balled his hand up into a fist and struck Ronald viciously against the head.

"Wait, man, wait," Ronald began to plead, "I'll give you back the money he gave his daughter. I was just takin' it to put in the bank for her!"

The man's words made no sense to Earl. He had a job to do and speed was the best thing. Before he could wrap his huge hands around Ronald's neck, the boy managed to scream. It was a high, piercing sound that carried the fear he felt. He knew he was facing death.

He struggled against the hands that held him but it was useless. It was as though he was in the grip of an iron machine. Nothing he did could make the animal-like man in front of him let go. Ronald tried to kick, but again his action was in vain.

Earl lifted the smaller man off his feet as he applied pressure to the boy's neck. The kicks that Ronald used against him just seemed to bounce off Earl's legs. He twisted his body around so that Ronald couldn't kick him between the legs.

The high scream that Ronald had let out put a cold block of

fear in Janet's heart. From her apartment she knew at once that it was Ronald. It was a feeling she had. Grabbing up a housecoat and tossing it around her shoulders, she ran to the door of her apartment and flung it open. As she ran down the hallway, she saw the two men struggling, moving as though they were in slow motion.

"Earl," she screamed at the top of her voice as she came near. The sound of her voice only added strength to the giant's hands. He gave one final shake of the boy's neck and was rewarded for his trouble by hearing a snap. He knew he had succeeded in doing what he had come to do. He had broken the boy's neck.

Ronald was like a doll in his arms. He tossed the useless body away from him as Janet came running up. At the sight of the mutilated body, she let out another scream. This one began on a high note and seemed to swell.

Earl took one quick glance over his shoulder at her and ran. He hadn't wanted her to see him, but it was too late now. Either way, it was over and done with. He took the stairway down three steps at a time. Before he reached the first floor, the outer door opened and two blue-uniformed policemen came walking in.

The first thing they heard was the screaming from Janet, then the next thing they knew, a huge black man came roaring down the steps. With one sweep of his huge arms, Earl knocked one of the officers completely off his feet. The other policeman just took a glancing blow, then he came back off the wall clutching at his gun.

Still running, Earl was at the outer door when the policeman's warning reached him. It had no immediate effect on the running man. If he had understood, he wouldn't have stopped. The first bullet caught him in his back but didn't even slow him down. He was out the doorway and on his way when the policeman took careful aim and fired again. His next bullet struck the fleeing man in the neck, hitting the huge main vein.

When the bullet came out on the other side, a gush of blood followed it.

Earl still remained on his feet. He fell against a car and balanced himself. As he started to run again, the policeman took aim and fired once more. This time the bullet struck him high in the back and staggered him until he fell.

After running back to her apartment intending to call an ambulance for Ronald, Janet heard the shooting and raced to her front window. She was in time to see Earl fall on his face. But she also saw someone else.

She saw Daddy Cool, who had just pulled up and gotten out of his car. When she looked out, her father was running toward the big man. She thought at once that he had been there all the time. More than likely he had put the huge man up to doing what he had done, she reasoned.

With tears flowing down her cheeks, Janet wished with all her heart that her father would have just waited. Now she could never forgive him. If only he would have let her work it out, she was sure he would have been happy.

Now, it was all over and she knew that Ronald was dead out in the hallway. And the responsibility for it was downstairs kneeling on the sidewalk, the only person to come out of this smelling like a rose.

It was something she couldn't allow him to get away with. With slow deliberation, Janet began to dress. When she finished, she opened the drawer and removed two of the long-bladed knives. After concealing them under her jacket, she started for the door.

Downstairs, Daddy Cool knelt beside the huge man. "Why, why, Earl, why didn't you wait for me, old-timer? Then none of this would have happened." Daddy Cool leaned down and held the huge man's head. Blood from the man's wounds soaked his clothes, but Daddy Cool didn't pay any heed to it. There were honest tears in his eyes as he held his close friend, staring down at the huge man as the last flicker of life left his eyes. At the last moment, Earl tried to say something, but he wasn't able to get the words out.

The policeman who had done the shooting approached the slain man. "You knew this guy?" he inquired as his partner came running up.

"Yeah," Larry Jackson answered, "he worked for me."

"Well, he killed a guy with his hands in the hallway," the other policeman said.

"Yeah, I know," Daddy Cool replied. He didn't have to see the body to know. He had seen Ronald's car, and had put two and two together. As he got up and straightened out his hurting knees from the concrete, he wondered how his daughter would take this. More than likely she would end up holding me responsible, Daddy Cool reflected.

"Say, we'd like to get a statement from you," one of the policemen said.

"From me?" Daddy Cool answered sharply, then laughed. "Hell, man, I'm not the one who shot him. See your partner there," he stated as he saw his daughter come out of the doorway.

She was staring straight ahead. Her eyes came to rest on his face, and she never looked away. Oh shit, Daddy Cool said to himself as he waited for her. It's like I thought. She thinks I'm responsible for this shit! He had to smile as he watched her close the distance between them. She's so much like I used to be, he thought as he looked at her with pride.

When her hand went under her jacket and she came out with the knife, he smiled again. He had known she would come up with it before she revealed it. The movement had been smooth and easy. He took pride in her experience.

I wonder if I could beat her from here, he reflected as he watched her hand go back. In a detached way, it seemed as if she was doing it to someone else, and he was on a stage watching. If she kills me straight out, he reflected in his last seconds, she'll end up facing a first-degree murder charge.

With that thought in mind, he decided to make his move. Not to hurt her, but only to protect her from the long arm of the law. He knew he still had three of his own weapons on him.

"You're wrong, Janet," he screamed loudly, then made his move. She had too much of a head start though, and he knew it. She was good, but he believed that it would have been easy for him to take her. He flipped the knife from out of his shoulder rig, but it was too late.

Already death was winging its way through the air. He didn't try to dodge the knife throw. He just hoped the police saw it as self-defense for his girl. She would need all the help she could get. But instead of throwing the knife, he held it in his hand.

At the last instant, he knew he would have had plenty of time to get his toss off.

If he had really wanted to.

Books by Donald Goines available in paperback from Holloway House, the original publishers of *Daddy Cool.*

Black Gangster
Black Girl Lost
Crime Partners
Cry Revenge
Death List
Dopefiend
Eldorado Red
Inner City Hoodlum
Kenyatta's Escape
Kenyatta's Last Hit
Never Die Alone
Street Players
Swamp Man
White Justice; Black Brief
Whoreson